Dead Solid Perfect

Dead Solid Perfect

Dan Jenkins

ANCHOR BOOKS

A Division of Random House, Inc.

New York

FIRST ANCHOR BOOKS (BROADWAY BOOKS) EDITION, 2001

Grateful acknowledgment is made for the use of excerpts from these songs:

"Gettin' By" and "Curly and Lil," words and music by
Jerry Jeff Walker. Published by Groper Music, Inc. BMI.
Lyrics reprinted by permission.

"Low Down Freedom," words and music by Billy Joe Shaver.
Copyright © 1971 ATV Music Corp. All rights controlled and
administered by Blackwood Music, Inc. under license from ATV Music.
All rights reserved. International copyright secured.
Lyrics reprinted by permission.

The Library of Congress Cataloging-in-Publication Data has cataloged the
Doubleday edition as:

Jenkins, Dan.
Dead solid perfect / by Dan Jenkins.—1st ed.
p.   cm.
"A Main Street book"—T.p. verso.
1. Golf—Fiction. I. Title.
PS3560.E4 D4 2000
813'.54—dc21

Anchor ISBN: 978-0-385-49885-2

www.anchorbooks.com

Printed in the United States of America
11 10 9 8 7

For the old house on Travis Avenue
and all the love that was inside of it.

Contents

Foreword

T his is a novel that didn't know when its time
was. So I am greatly pleased and delighted and
even breaking into grins to see it put back in
circulation, purely for its educational value, of course.

It came out about fifteen years too early, like
ahead of the golf boom. I'm not exactly sure when the
golf boom began—I suppose it had something to do with
the invention of Big Bertha in 1991, the club that started
the craze in oversized metal drivers.

All I know is, everybody in the world who
wasn't a golfer suddenly took up golf one day, loved it,
and started saying things like, "I cold-striped it, man. I
mean, I clubfaced it. I pured that sumbitch so dead solid
perfect, the honey ran down my leg, and I money-
whipped ever-swingin' dick on the dance floor."

I'm not complaining. When the novel first

appeared in 1974 it did well enough for me to buy dinner at Elaine's one night, which wasn't a bad deal when you consider that the only golf book anybody had read back then was Ben Hogan's *Five Lessons: The Modern Fundamentals of Golf.*

Go out on a golf course in those days and you couldn't find a software executive anywhere, much less a real estate broker, criminal lawyer, fine arts major, diesel mechanic, consciousness-raising geek, or young mother.

Now everybody you know plays golf, joins five country clubs, and buys titanium like buttered popcorn in a movie about teenage mutants, which is most movies today.

Not only that. At least half of these instant golf nuts are writing books about the game and miraculously getting them published by naive or demented editors who've also taken up golf in the last thirty minutes.

Well, you could cover me over with sand in your deepest bunker before I'd bother to read any of them, especially if the author is someone that nobody remotely connected with golf has ever heard of, but I do stare at the books with bewilderment when they happen to be sitting on the shelves of the various Barnes & Deli stores I frequent.

Such current works as:

My Brain and Your Swing by Dr. Happy Rotate.

Divots in the Office Carpet by Owen Slasher.

I Was a 16 from the Whites by C. L. Smithwick, accountant.

Golf in the Haggis by Murky Arcane.

A Good Major Spoiled by I. M. Boring.

The Legend of Dad, Jones, Hagen, Jesus and Me at Pine Valley on That Mystical Day by Dodge Fader.

Those books and others like them have inspired a new one I'm working on. It's a mystery thriller. I'm calling it, *Who's Killing All the Bad Golf Writers in America?*

But let's talk about *Dead Solid Perfect* for a moment, since it's the most authentic golf book I've ever read—or written.

At the time it was based on my twenty-five years—it's up to fifty years now—of covering big-time pro golf for newspapers and magazines.

You can say things in fiction that you can't say in journalism, of course. Get closer to the truth.

Thus, if you care to know what it's really like out there on the PGA Tour, or at a major championship such as the U.S. Open—on and off the course—I shamelessly recommend it.

Hey, if you don't like such characters as Kenny Lee Puckett and Donny Smithern and Grover Scomer, then you just don't like golf.

And if you don't like such ladies as Beverly Tidwell and Janie Ruth Rimmer, then you just don't like shapely adorables.

Okay. End of commercial. Gentlemen, play away.

—Dan Jenkins, 1999

87th

U.S. Open Golf Championship

June 15–21

GUEST

Clubhouse & Grounds

NOT TRANSFERABLE

HEAVENLY PINES COUNTRY CLUB

HEAVENLY, N. C.

NOTE: Please wear this badge at all times in plain view of the guards and attendants in order to avoid embarrassment to the Committee, the Sponsors, the Members, the Contestants, and yourself.

Part 1

*Air Travel, Pretty Girls
and Happiness*

One

WHEN I CAME OFF the golf course that first afternoon a bunch of those TV phonies captured me and I had to go on camera and talk to a guy in a safari suit who looked like he'd just set a new Southern regional hair-spray record. Captain Big Voice, I called him. He was a dandy little jewel. I don't know how I missed marrying him. I married everybody else who stood still long enough. Like one of my intellectual buddies back in Texas used to say, "Kenny, anything you can't fuck up, you'll shit on."

After I made it over to the press tent I told the sports writers I was sorry to be so late, particularly since I was among the tournament leaders. But I'd been trapped by a television interviewer who sat down and crossed his legs, lit up a brushed-denim Winston, and recited everything he knew about golf except the history of the alpaca sweater.

"Not but two things in the world I don't do about your TV," I said to the writers. "And both of 'em are care."

I figured I'd try to be as amusing as possible for the "Working Press." It's good public relations, they say, to dress up the literary folks.

I said, "Hell, men, when I finally got a chance to squeeze a word in on the old six o'clock news, I couldn't resist telling everybody about the screamin'est damn 1-iron anybody every hit."

On the last fairway I'd caught this 1-iron just perfect and bored a hole through the wind. Finished up the round with a birdie three on a par-four hole that's nothing but two miles of lonesome road.

In case you don't know very much about the game of golf, a good 1-iron shot is about as easy to come by as an understanding wife. And a birdie on a tough hole like the 18th at Heavenly Pines is a hell of a lot better than diarrhea. Especially when you're playing in a tournament like the Open Championship of the United States, which is a dignified way to refer to the National Open—the biggest event there is.

As I said in the press tent, "Man, I crawled on that shot like an eighteen-wheel rig rollin' down I 35. Just wore it out. And the minute the ball started for that flagstick I knew the war was over and it was time to call in the boats and piss on the admiral."

I hauled out a few other expressions from my gambling days in Texas. Said I'd hit one shot out there—a wind cheater—that was lower to the ground than a Louisiana mud varmint. That damn golf course we were trying to play, old Heavenly Pines, was stronger than rent, I said. And when I got about halfway through the first round of the Open on Thursday, I started thinking, "Oh, Lord, I don't want the cheese, I just want out of the trap."

And now for your listening pleasure, I said, here's a little song I wrote one day in divorce court. Tells you something about my past. It's called "If My Heart's Community Property Then Get Your Mental Cruelty Off My Ass."

Incidentally, I suppose I ought to explain what I do for a living. I play golf, is what I do. I mean, that's it. I'm a touring pro.

What this means is, I can play the game good enough to be a member of something called the Tournament Players Division of the Professional Golfers Association of America. It shouldn't take more than thirty seconds to get all of that out of your mouth.

See, there's this thing out there in America known as the PGA tour. It's a whole pile of golf tournaments— about forty of them, in fact—that are held week after week, all over the country, in which about 150 guys like me compete for roughly $24 million in total prize money every year.

Fuckin' gypsies are what we are. Except we use deodorant.

We start off the first week of January in California and then we pretty much keep on traveling around until it all ends up sometime in October. Then we rest a couple of months and do it all over again. It's back to all those glamour spots like Pebble Beach, Honolulu, New

Orleans, Las Vegas, Miami, and Palm Springs, and twice as many Akrons, Greensboros, and Fort Worths.

After a while you realize you've been in so many motels you think your name is Ramada.

I wouldn't recommend the life if you don't like highways and air-travel cards. But of course you're playing a game for a living. Never knew very many golf pros who had to slip into some coveralls and try to repair a washer-dryer or unstop a toilet.

The thing is, you don't even have to win any of these tournaments to come out all right financially. You can just go along finishing fifth or tenth or fifteenth or twenty-fourth every week, and you'll earn enough to keep yourself in cashmeres and a Lincoln Continental that won't overheat in traffic.

Hell, I'm a good example. Kenny Lee Puckett, white man, thirty-four. Compared to your basic millionaire like Jack Nicklaus, I'm nobody. But I can win myself about $200,000 a year if I can just manage to thump the ball around with my dick.

I'm fairly certain that the average sports fan gets bored with all these tournaments we play. So do we at times, except for the money. What I mean is, there's your sports fan at home with his TV, his beer, and his Velveeta on rye, ready to watch some action on the old portable Sony. But here comes the Greater Hartford Open on the screen, and it looks just like the Greater Memphis Open the week before and the Greater Atlanta Classic the week before that. So the sports fan hollers at his wife:

"God damn, Charlene, switch that thing over to another channel so we can watch some niggers play ball—

or at least see a bunch of Frenchmen get killed in a car race."

Well, there are four different occasions a year, at least, when it gets kind of special. Not only for the public but also for the press and the players. That's when a "major championship" comes up. I'm talking about the Masters in April, down there in Augusta, Georgia, or the National Open in June, like they were holding at Heavenly Pines, or the British Open every July, or the National PGA in August.

A touring pro wouldn't do anything more than trade his wife, kids, mistress, and all of the Milwaukee Opens he'd won in the past for any one of the Big Four. Just to win one of them—once—can make his whole career worthwhile. Especially the National Open.

The glory is a big part of it, sure. But a shrewd fellow can also turn a major championship into a million dollars through endorsements, exhibitions, affiliations, and all of that fringe-benefit stuff.

As a matter of fact, just to be in contention for one of the big ones is quite an experience, which I found out about at Heavenly Pines. It'll get you more publicity and attention over three or four days than you could scare up in five months of rape.

By the way, this PGA tour I'm trying to describe didn't exactly get started yesterday. A lot of people probably think it came about when a family named Palmer turned up with a son named Arnold out there in Latrobe, Pennsylvania.

Actually, the tour began to evolve about sixty years ago, back in the 1920's, and sort of by accident, really.

PART 1

What happened was, a few pros decided they suddenly knew how to play the game better than the rich amateurs they worked for in country clubs around Newport and Easthampton and Atlantic City, or wherever there were a lot of wealthy fuckers in white suits and straw hats.

These pros had familiar names like Walter Hagen and Gene Sarazen and Tommy Armour. They'd take off from their club jobs in the winter and go to Florida and California and Texas, jack the ball up in a contest, and pass the hat.

It turned out that people around several hotels and resorts and real estate developments enjoyed watching them. So a few promoters stepped in and figured out that you could make a resort or a hotel or a country club just as famous with a golf tournament as you could with a fire.

Now pro golf had a circus to sell. And fortunately some new stars kept on coming. In the 1930's and 1940's it was Ben Hogan and Byron Nelson and Sam Snead and Jimmy Demaret. And at the same time a lot more towns and resorts and clubs and hotels began putting up more money for the circus.

Then came that thing the Palmer family of Latrobe, Pennsylvania, did. In the late 1950's and the early 1960's their boy, Arnold, was all grown up—and so was television. And mainly because of Arnold the tournament purses started to double, and then triple.

Everybody wanted to see Arnold. He chain-smoked, sweated, frowned, let his shirttail hang out, tossed his visor in the air, and tried to hit the ball through a tree

8

trunk with a golf swing that looked like it came out of a mine shaft. And he dressed like a guy who might have been tailored by a dry-goods store in Latrobe.

But he beat the crap out of everybody, and he took the game to the masses.

That kind of brings us up to now and this $24 million out here for people like me to play for. Or anybody else who's good enough to get through the PGA's qualifying school, and who's either got the money or the sponsor to bankroll himself on the tour.

I guess I ought to explain one other thing. There's no guarantee you'll win money out here. It's true that normally 150 players start out on a 72-hole tournament for about $500,000, but after the first two rounds only the low seventy scorers get to continue on over the last two days for the prize money. The others have missed the 36-hole cut and gone C.O.D. that week. They've hopped in their cars, or on planes, and headed for the next tournament and a few quiet dinners with Mr. Ramada.

Every week's a new ball game though. There's always the hope you'll play good and stick your hand about six inches up the golden goose's ass. That's why we're all out here, being gypsies who smell good.

Now if you ask me why so many people want to put up so much money for us to compete for, I can't give you a sensible answer. There's no law that says there has to be a golf tour.

If all the sponsors got together and decided they were weary of seeing us every year, it would all be over. Most of us would have to sit down on the curb and learn how to play the harmonica, or something.

9

PART 1

This won't ever happen, of course. And I suppose the reason is because the golf pro has somehow figured out how to do something pretty well, consistently, that seems close to impossible to a lot of rich spastics.

For one thing, that sure is a small ball you're trying to swing at. And it sure is a long way to that green. And when you get there that cup is not exactly as big as a corporation president's ego.

Actually, all I'm trying to say is, I'm happy to be a part of it. I think I'm fortunate, although I'm aware that golf is probably some kind of a mental disorder like gambling or women or politics.

But it happens to be a disease I got afflicted with early. Aged nine, I think. Or whenever it was that I saw my first photograph of a golf pro, all slick and pretty, in a knit shirt, a pair of unborn-billy-goat shoes, and some pants that didn't seem to have a belt.

A golf course always looked like a better place for a man to be than underneath a car with a wrench in his hand, or behind a desk trying to read the fine print on something that had to be notarized.

If you were a golf pro, I decided, whether you were good enough to play the tour or not, it wouldn't matter if the damned old sun didn't rise. You could just reach up and switch on the light.

Anyhow, it worked out that I just never tried to learn much about anything other than the game of golf.

I mean, all I know about the real world—or what you call your commerce—is that some guys sell little ones, some guys sell big ones, some of it comes in on trains and some of it goes out in barges, a guy named Irving is

10

locked up in a closet somewhere to figure it all out, most of it adds up to an argument in a courtroom, and all the people who're lucky enough to be hanging around drinking at all the country clubs get to shit on everybody else.

When a pro shoots a score that's low enough to get him invited to the press tent, the first thing he's expected to do is describe his round, hole by hole. That's so any of the writers who haven't been out on the course will know what happened. Quite a few noted authors seem to prefer hanging around the clubhouse bars, or the locker room, or looking at geese on the verandas.

Going through the round, you find yourself saying things like, "Second hole . . . driver . . . wedge . . . two putts from twenty-five feet. Third hole . . . three-iron . . . blew it from eight feet."

This enables the writers to tell about it for their readers as if they saw you play the shots, and America gets to find out what happened that day in the grand old game that Mary Queen of Scots invented.

Occasionally somebody will ask a player to go into more detail on a specific shot. That's when you might have a chance to say something colorful like Lee Trevino does pretty often.

For example, the Mex might say, "I hit that son of a bitch so straight you could hang laundry on it."

And in the morning paper the next day you might see a headline that would say:

TREVINO CREDITS 'LAUNDRY' SHOT FOR DORAL LEAD.

As I mentioned earlier, I tried to make the most of my visit to the press tent on Thursday at Heavenly Pines. It was the first time I'd ever been in there during the National Open. I'd played in the Open before, of course. Several times. And I'd been in all of the other majors now and then. But I'd never been any closer to the lead than the parking lot.

Not that a few of the writers didn't know me. I mean, I'd been out there a while—like about eight years. And I'd been making money, as I say. But to the bulk of your press corps, I was just set decoration. One of those guys who plugged along and maybe won himself a Pensacola Open every year or two.

I sure wasn't any Jack Nicklaus or Lee Trevino or Arnold Palmer, or even Tom Watson or Ben Crenshaw. Not even a Donny Smithern, who was one of my closest pals on the tour, and who also happened to be in contention at Heavenly Pines.

Anyhow, after I'd finished going through my round the writers wanted to find out some personal stuff about me. Somebody handed me another beer while I sat up there on a platform in the tent behind a microphone and stared out at about a hundred guys with notebooks.

I said, "I want all of you to know that I'm one of the most important people in golf. Jack Nicklaus has to have *somebody* to beat."

Then I provided a little background for the writers who didn't know me so well.

As for the tournaments I'd won, I said, there hadn't been anything more important than the Bad Breath Invitation three years ago, and the Body Odor Classic last year.

That got some laughter.

I said I was born in Fort Worth, Texas, the All-American town. Red, white, and blue. Home of the redneck, the white undershirt, and the blue norther. Said it happened to be the town that also gave you Ben Hogan and Byron Nelson—fore, please. But I said if I had anything in common with those two gentlemen, I couldn't imagine what it was. Other than the fact that all of us might remember Fort Worth as a place where you still had to stop for freight trains no matter where you were going in your car.

Said I'd basically developed my game on an old public course in Fort Worth called Goat Hills. Which also happened to be where I learned a considerable amount about gambling, thieves, 102-degree heat, copperheads, rocks, dirt, and gourmet food.

"The all-time winner on the menu in the Goat Hills lunchroom," I said, "was a grease sandwich on light bread with brown-speckled lettuce."

Thought I was mildly hilarious when I pointed out that I *did* have something in common with Jack Nicklaus, however. During my career, I said, I had skillfully managed to accumulate the same number of wives as Nicklaus had won British Opens. Three.

I apologized to the writers for having birdied that last hole on Thursday. It gave me a 71 and tied me for the lead with a couple of better-knowns, Hale Irwin and Lanny Wadkins.

"Maybe I'll take gas before Sunday like a Nobody should, and you won't have to mess around with me," I said, faking a smile.

One of the writers who knew me asked how it felt to have my good buddy, Donny Smithern, only one stroke behind me. Donny had opened up with a 72.

That question got some of the other writers excited. Here were these wonderful old pals—Smithern and Puckett—right up there to fight it out for the National Open.

I said, "We've got a lot of golf to play before this thing's over. Neither one of us might be important to you fellows in a couple more days."

Somebody wanted to know how close Donny and I were.

That wasn't easy to answer. I felt like saying I personally didn't know any two players on the tour who were so close they could both fart in the same Coke bottle.

But what I said was, "Donny was one of the first guys I met when I came out here. I think he recognized that I was a sneaky good player. And he thought he could take me for a partner and maybe we could rob some guys in practice rounds."

Players do enjoy a wager now and then in practice. Just to keep the competitive edge, you understand.

I explained that Donny and I had traveled together some, with and without our wives. But I said Donny was among the elite. He'd won a couple of major championships. He was what you called established. He'd won the Open before, for one thing, at Deer Run. And he'd won the PGA, too, at Quail Hollow.

I said, hell, Donny was almost on the same level with those guys who travel with a business manager, a valet, a nurse, a tax consultant, a secretary, a press agent, and a copilot. One more big one for Donny, I said, and he would be sitting around on all the network talk shows pretending that he thought the Middle East was something besides an NCAA basketball play-off.

To be honest I didn't know what to tell the writers about Donny and me. We *were* friends. But somehow that friendship had a tendency to lose quite a bit of warmth when Tom Watson, or anybody more important than me, walked into a room and asked Donny to come have a drink or go to dinner.

I'd met Donny in Los Angeles at my very first pro tournament. This was when they played the L.A. Open at Rancho Park before they moved it to Riviera. I remember I was out on the practice tee, beating balls, when Donny walked up and stood there watching me. He must have decided he liked my action, because he spoke to me.

"Got a game?" he said. It was Tuesday, a warm-up day.

He didn't ask what my name was, and he *assumed* I knew who he was.

I said I didn't have a game.

He said, "I got Zark and Ruffin at one o'clock. Want to play 'em?"

I thought about that. Rex Zark and Eddie Ruffin. Good players. Tournament winners. Names.

I said, "What kind of game do you guys play?"

"I'll be the bookkeeper," Donny said. "You just make some birdies."

"I played good yesterday," I said.

"Yesterday ain't for shit," said Donny. "Let me see you hit that driver. Looks like you might be pretty long."

I hit a tee ball for him.

"You'll do," he said. "You've got to be from Texas with that accent."

Fort Worth, I told him.

"I was at Colonial last year," he said. "Should have won."

"Yeah," I said. "I saw you fuck it up on seventeen."

He said, "I'd like to turn the Corps of Engineers loose on that shitheel place."

I grinned.

He asked what my name was. We shook hands. Then he said we'd play Zark and Ruffin a $50 Nassau. Automatic one-down presses. I said that was pretty strong for me. He said he'd take my half. I said, naw, I didn't travel that way.

"Then I'd suggest you play your ass off," he said.

I did, luckily. And we sheared Zark and Ruffin for about $600 each, which was considerably more than I won in the L.A. Open.

Donny asked me what I was doing that evening.

I said I didn't know too many movie stars. I guessed I wasn't doing anything.

"Yeah, you are," he said. "You and me are driving down to Manhattan Beach and see how many stewardesses are sad and lonely."

He said there weren't more than three or four million

16

stews who lived in Manhattan Beach and liked to wander around in the night.

I said, "Well, there ought to be several who'd be just tickled to death to stumble onto a couple of eccentric rich fellows like you and me."

Donny smiled and said:

"I may let you hang around awhile."

Our evening in Manhattan Beach was fairly uneventful from my point of view. We went to this large barn that had a bar, a dance floor, a group of musicians from an undiscovered planet, and all of the girls Donny had promised.

All I did was drink and listen while he told several different tales to several different girls named Marilyn and Stephanie and I've forgotten what else. I heard that Donny's wife, Katie, was a polio victim. I heard she was a heart patient. Once I think I heard she had actually died of leukemia.

We wound up in some girl's small apartment near the ocean where I scrambled eggs for everybody while Donny and the girl performed some naked acrobatics on the living room sofa.

When I walked in to serve the eggs, Donny said, "We're in love."

I said, "Oh, well, that's okay, then. For a minute I thought it was The Flying Punzars."

Later on, driving back up to L.A., I asked Donny if his wife traveled with him often.

"Katie?" he said. "Sure. She'll be in Phoenix next week. *Super* lady. I really got lucky when I picked Katie out of the litter."

From that day and night on, Donny and I were frequent partners in the practice games and decent enough
friends, considering that our private conversations were
nearly always limited to the only two subjects Donny
cared about: golf and cunt.

In the press tent at Heavenly Pines the writers probed
slightly into my domestic life. All I told them was that
Janie Ruth was my third wife—old number three—and
that we had been married about two years. I pointed out
that Janie Ruth had been the one in my gallery wearing
a pair of shorts and a halter that could have gotten her
arrested, the girl in the mirrored glasses with the long
red hair tumbling down her shoulders.

If any of the writers had seen her out on the course,
then they surely knew I didn't need to say that Janie
Ruth was also the young lady luggin' around all those
tits.

I certainly didn't need to tell the press what Donny
had said after Janie Ruth and I were married. He'd said:

"You can't ever play in a tournament outside the country, Kenny, because Janie Ruth'll never get those things
through customs."

As for the two previous wives, I think all I said to the
writers was that Joy Needham, old number one, was
simply a part of my wondrous high school and college
days. And Beverly Tidwell, old number two, was just
one of those mistakes a man can make when he marries a
rich intellectual.

I suppose I did mention that, as far as I could tell, it
might not be possible for any man to be married to
Beverly Tidwell unless he was a Nobel Prize-winning

poet who could also handle any household problems that came up involving plumbing or electrical wiring.

Before I got out of the press tent that Thursday I was asked to go into some detail about a pretty bizarre thing which happened to me during the round. A golf ball had exploded on me.

I had heard of it happening before, but I hadn't seen it until I hit a tee ball on the 14th hole at Heavenly Pines. Hell of a time. Right there in the National Open.

The way you know a ball has exploded is that it doesn't stay in the air very long after you've hit it. It takes a sharp curve, one way or another, and dives into the ground. What's happened is, the center of it has cracked because of a manufacturing defect. You can replace the ball with a new one, of course, but you've lost distance on the shot.

I told the writers that after I'd hit the drive, Janie Ruth came over to the gallery ropes and hollered at me, wondering what the devil had gone on.

My caddy, Roosevelt, said to her, "Boss done hit a voodoo ball."

When I reached the ball a short way up the fairway I replaced it, and then I went over to the ropes and handed the one with the cracked center to Janie Ruth. It was like mush. You could squeeze it together.

Janie Ruth mashed on it.

Roosevelt said if nobody wanted it he'd like to keep it as a souvenir of the Open.

"God damn, take it," Janie Ruth said. "It's soft as one of them Pillsbury refrigerated biscuits you shake out of a can."

I'd repeated her remark to the press. The writers were

fascinated, naturally. And I was reasonably sure that in some newspaper the following day there would be a headline which said:

PUCKETT SURVIVES 'BISCUIT BALL.'

Totaling all of it up I supposed that I strolled out of the press tent satisfied that I had been an unexpectedly good interview.

There's no question that Janie Ruth had been good for my golf at that time. She was easy to be with. She liked the sport. At least she thought all the travel was glamorous. She seemed to understand me.

She was just about everything that Beverly Tidwell had never been. As far as my golf game was concerned.

I can remember saying to Donny Smithern and Grover Scomer one day, "Man, you can look behind every great player and you'll find a good woman."

All of the pros agreed that a Barbara Nicklaus or a Winnie Palmer or a Jeanne Weiskopf—and several others—had a lot to do with the success of their husbands. But we also agreed that if a man had to live with one of those unraked bunkers, like some guys did, it was a heavy load.

"A bad wife'll strap a terminal hook on you," Donny said once. "You can just start walking left every time you swing the club."

My first wife out of the box—Joy Needham—didn't have any effect on my golf, but of course I was only a hustler then in Fort Worth. It didn't matter.

Joy was a good-looking thing from high school. She

was plenty good-hearted, too. But she had this minor problem. She couldn't stay out of a motel room with any guy who was a good dancer or drove fast or told her a dirty joke.

I got rid of Joy Needham long before I ever came out here.

Naw, the one that was tough on my psyche, or whatever you call it, was Beverly Tidwell. Old Bev furnished the living proof that a man ought to beware of wives who think they're wiser in all ways than their husbands.

When Beverly was on the tour with me I felt like she stayed on my ass about everything from the color schemes I wore to who we were going to have dinner with. And because of how she made me feel—whether she meant to or not—I'll bet I spent more time in the fuckin' trees than Robin Hood.

I've kind of changed my mind about something in the last few months, however. I think I would have made it out here even if I'd stayed married to Beverly. It wouldn't have been as much fun as a Tex/Mex dinner, but I would have survived and still become a money winner.

I could play this old game a little, even when I first came out here. I'd played it good enough around Goat Hills and elsewhere in Texas to get me enough money together that I didn't have to go ass-kiss a sponsor to send me out.

And I stayed. Right from that first L.A. Open where I met Donny. Didn't have to give up and go take a job at a driving range or anything.

I'd hustled up about $15,000 to start off with, figuring

if I ate enough candy bars I could play half the year. But
I won some checks right away. I believe my "official"
money the first year was something like $27,000, but I
know Donny and I won at least that much—tax free—on
Tuesdays before the tournaments ever started.

Like I say, the good thing about this was that I didn't
have to go crawling back to Fort Worth to beg some of
the rich guys around the country clubs to sponsor me for
fifty percent of my winnings.

A sponsor is a good deal for a young player who hasn't
got any other way to get out here. If the sponsor will
agree to turn loose of him after the player makes it on his
own. What the sponsor will do is give the kid some plastic and about $500 in cash a week, and at the end of the
year they'll sit down and balance his expenses against his
winnings. Maybe the sponsor makes money, maybe he
breaks even, maybe he gets a deduction. Meanwhile, the
young player's been on the tour.

I got approached by an oil man in Fort Worth when
word got around that I might be thinking about coming
out here. His name was Joe Ralph Rucker. He picked his
teeth with money.

He summoned me to lunch one day at River Crest
Country Club and sat me down with himself and a few
cocktails. I knew him. He thought he could play golf
some, but he couldn't play so good that he needed to
carry around as much money as he always did. I'd been
in his pocket.

"Kenny," he said, "you're a good player, but there's lots
of those. Understand what I'm talkin' about?"

I thought I did.

Joe Ralph Rucker said, "You're about the best around here right now. But you ain't played too much outside of Texas, have you?"

That was true, I said. I'd been to Oklahoma, parts of Louisiana, and the Mexican border. That was about it.

"That golf tour," he said, "goes lots of places where they got grass and trees and water and hills."

"Don't you get a free drop off the grass?" I said, being funny.

Joe Ralph Rucker got down to it.

He said, "Kenny, you got length. That's a big thing. I don't know where you get it 'cause you ain't that big, but you're long. I heard you clean drove the 11th at Goat Hills one day. Is that right?"

There'd been a big wind, I said.

"Here's what I want to do," he said. "By god, I think what you're up to is just as damned American as an editorial in the *Oil & Gas Journal*. But I want to give you a little insurance."

I asked him what he had in mind.

He said, "I'm gonna send you out there so that you don't have to worry about nothin' but hittin' that long ball. What do you need? Five thousand for a couple of months? Ten thousand for three or four?"

I asked Joe Ralph Rucker what he wanted out of the deal.

"Aw, hell, fun's all," he said. "I don't own no race horses. You're gonna be my race horse, I guess. As for the business aspect . . . well . . . if you happen to start winnin' . . . why don't we just do the normal sixty-forty split?"

PART 1

Who was the sixty, I asked?

"I've checked into that," he said. "It's the sponsor, actually. Only proper, I suppose. Man puts up the money
gets the biggest return. But, hell. Don't worry about
that. You just play good."

I thanked Joe Ralph Rucker for the offer and the
drinks. But I said I thought I might try it on my own.

He said, "You sure you know what you're sayin'? I'm
talkin' about eatin' steak and playin' golf. I'm talkin'
about ever day bein' a holiday."

I was sure, I said.

He sat there for a minute. Then he said:

"Well, I admire you, and I wish you luck. And let me
say this. If there's ever anything anybody in Fort Worth
can do for you . . . just give us a holler out here at River
Crest."

I said I appreciated it, but River Crest had done
enough for me already, making me want to get out of
town.

Joe Ralph Rucker didn't clearly hear me. He was busy
yelling at somebody across the room about some drilling
pipe spinning off at 7500 feet out in Scogie County.

The nearest I ever came to needing any financial help
on the tour was when I was locked in all of that marital
bliss with Beverly Tidwell. Bev was a special person, but
she just never should have married a golfer.

Of course she always said I was more than that.
Which was part of our problem. I didn't want to be. So I
spent four years with her wondering what I was, or
wasn't, or should be—and trying to play the tour.

I'm not sure it was my profession which finally broke
us up. After a while it didn't matter what the cause was.

24

I just didn't have the energy it took to compete, practice, travel, and devote my free time to all of the debates Bev seemed to enjoy.

We lived in an apartment in Dallas, which is where I'd met her. Quite a few pros live in Dallas. Donny and Katie did at the time. They had a big, nice house on the good side of town—north—which Donny sprung for after he'd won his first major championship.

There are three or four reasons why a lot of pros choose Dallas as a nest. The airline service is good. You can go either way, and get there faster, because you're centrally located. There are good courses to practice on, like Brook Hollow, Northwood, and Preston Trail. It's cheaper than either coast. And quite a number of pros somehow wind up marrying stewardesses from the area.

Bev was not a Dallas-lover, although it was her hometown. She said it was a "dumb, pretentious city" which thought of itself as "a miniature New York with symphonies instead of Puerto Ricans."

The day I moved out of the apartment she had been trying to argue with me about—I think—"the ethical decay of corporate America." While I casually carried things to the car.

"You know," I said, "you thrive on combat so much you should have been a fuckin' Israeli."

I was loading the usual single man's valuables into the trunk of the Lincoln Continental. A trophy lamp. Some record albums. Clothes. A fifteen-year-old autographed football with "City Champions" painted on it.

Bev said, "How shall one reach you in the future? In care of Smith, Barney?"

"Call the tour office," I said.

"Why do you give up so easily?" she said.

"Because I've never known what the hell I'm supposed to be fighting about."

What made the National Open at Heavenly Pines even more frustrating for me was Beverly's illness.

The thing is, it was the very week of the Open when I found out how serious Bev's condition was. Beautiful timing. I finally get in contention for a major championship and I find out that my ex-wife, who I don't hate—and who I actually have a tremendous fondness for—is in deep trouble with her lung.

Bev and I had managed to stay pals even after I'd married Janie Ruth. As far as that goes, Bev and I were probably better friends divorced than we ever were living together.

The first news I'd heard of Beverly's problem was earlier in the spring. She'd called me somewhere. Hilton Head, I think, during the Heritage Classic. Said she'd been moving some furniture around, got a pain in her back, went to a doctor, had an X-ray, and they'd discovered something not so terrific.

I was stunned. Bev was only thirty-one.

I'd said, "Hey, old buddy. They don't think it's anything silly, do they? Like . . . Big C . . . or any of his pals?"

"I may have to stop smoking," she said. "At least while the doctor's watching."

Janie Ruth had been underwhelmed with the news of Bev's illness. And if you stopped to think about where Janie Ruth came from—an old line of waitresses—you could partly understand why she might find it hard to feel much sympathy for somebody like Beverly Tidwell, whose family had some money. Even if that somebody might happen to be very sick.

When I told Janie Ruth that Bev had scared up this terrible situation in her lung, all she said was:

"Well, I don't waste much pity on anybody who's got more money than I do. If that smart-ass bitch dies, it ain't gonna move her up any."

● ● ●

Two

*I*HAVE ALWAYS THOUGHT IT was
ironic that I met Janie Ruth back in my
old hometown. I mean, there I was, a
guy who traveled all over the country playing the tour—
California, Florida, up East—and I had poured a little
wine for more than a few lovelies since I had separated
from Beverly, but it was right back in Fort Worth where
I met Janie Ruth.

It was about three years ago when I was there for the
Colonial. One night during the tournament me and
Donny Smithern and Grover Scomer decided to drive out
on the highway to a joint where we could hear some
country music.

We went to Dottie's Paradise, which was like most of
the country music places you run into. You wouldn't
want to be wearing any pastel colors when you walked in

there. Cowboys don't particularly like pastel colors on men.

The feature attraction turned out to be none other than Janie Ruth Rimmer, coming to you straight from a successful engagement as a cocktail waitress at Vernon Watson's Nip-'n-Sip just down the road.

She wasn't a bad singer. She could do a pretty solid Loretta Lynn imitation when she went with one of the goodies, like "Ain't No Two-Way Traffic in My Carport," or "Take Your Levi's Off My Chair."

We had just enough to drink that I sent a note up to the stage which said something on the order of, "How would a refined lady like yourself like to have a cocktail with several celebrities from the world of golf?"

Janie Ruth came over to our table between sets and captivated us with the number of cuss words she used— and a pair of All-Conference tits.

At first, I recall, Janie Ruth was more taken with Donny Smithern than with me. This was normal. Girls always seemed to rub up against Donny more regularly because he was a bigger "name" than Grover or me. Still is, for that matter.

Janie Ruth pretended she knew who all of us were. She even introduced us when she went back to the stage. Which was a good thing—and timely—because several of the truck drivers in Dottie's Paradise had been staring at Grover Scomer's checkered cottons.

Donny gave Janie Ruth a clubhouse badge for the rest of the tournament, and I gave her my contestant's parking sticker, and we told her to come on out to Colonial Country Club and hang around with the rich folks.

She wanted to know what she should wear to a golf tournament? We told her to dress comfortably. It had been hot.

Well, she turned up in a costume you could fold up and put inside of a menu. There wasn't anything to it but thighs and navels and tits. Some kind of tight shorts and a halter. I fuckin' near bogied three holes in a row when I saw her in my gallery the next day. And I think I wound up 38th in the tournament.

On the tour, of course, we all think of Colonial as the international headquarters for what we call "Hold Its." A Hold It is some kind of a lady strolling around with an impressive body and a look of merriment in her eyes. When you see a Hold It on the tour, at Colonial or anywhere else, you tend to turn quietly to the guy you're paired with and say:

"Uh, hold it. Hard left. Behind the front bunker. White pants. Red blouse. Wife Killer."

Janie Ruth's attitude about a golf tournament was fascinating. She couldn't understand why all of the crowds were so quiet.

In one of the clubhouse cocktail lounges that day she said:

"Hell, I thought I'd come out to a sports event. A damned old funeral's all this is."

She added, "Ain't no Dallas Cowboys around, or anybody who's any fun."

She kept looking around the room at various members of the tournament committee in their blazers and shirts and ties, and at one point she hollered:

"Ever-body wake up in here! Let's get with it!"

To liven things up, she decided to tell Donny and I a few jokes she thought were funny. They were mostly very old jokes about "niggers" and "Aggies" and "queers."

There was a moment when a fellow came over to the table where we were sitting. He was another one of those rich oil men, a guy named Ed Bookman, who had been the tournament chairman of Colonial for several years. If you were a true celebrity or almost as wealthy as he was, you would probably think he was a swell guy. You'd put him right up there with old Joe Ralph Rucker any day.

Janie Ruth was in the middle of another joke when the tournament chairman politely leaned down to her and said, "Excuse me, young lady, but I believe you're being just a bit obstreperous."

She hardly even glanced at him. She just half turned around and said, "Fuck off." And went on with her story.

For a few seconds the chairman looked as if somebody had hit him with a subpoena, but then he managed to grin. He winked at Donny and me like he had suddenly gotten a better view of Janie Ruth and realized she had a body that would make a man want to butt his head against a stump.

I suppose I knew right away that Janie Ruth Rimmer was somebody I wouldn't mind having around for a while. It's amazing what a woman's physical attributes can do to a man. So I put it right on her. I said why didn't she venture out on the tour? Said it didn't appear to me that she was likely to be soaring toward the top of the recording industry from Dottie's Paradise.

I said it just so happened that I was between pictures where wives were concerned. Said I had me a modest little Lincoln Continental with a tape deck, and I didn't go anywhere that wasn't all right. Pebble Beach and Pinehurst and those kind of low-rent districts.

I was honest. Told her I was still married to Beverly, which I was at the time. But I explained that I had been on the street for over six months and a divorce had been penciled in on my dance card.

Beverly and I had been married for three years, I said, but it had scarcely been what you would call your story-book romance.

"Bev's a neat girl," I said, "but she hates golf almost as much as she hates Wall Street."

I said Bev was attractive if you liked thin ones who wore glasses on top of their hair and preferred reading a few ghetto gazettes like *New York* magazine and *Rolling Stone* over *Sports Illustrated.*

Said I couldn't very well explain why Bev and I ever got married. It must have had something to do with the tour being such a lonely place. Sex might have played a minor character role in the drama, I said. It *was* different with Bev. Sort of like getting it on with the CBS Evening News. Or in the midst of a lecture on primitive arts and handicraft.

I even tried to answer the larger question of why Beverly Tidwell would marry *me.*

I must have been a welcome change from anyone she'd

ever known, I said. I didn't give a shit for Dallas, except that it was convenient. Bev liked that. I certainly didn't have any social aspirations, which she liked even more. The only debutantes I was familiar with charged $100 in the South and $200 on the Coast.

Frankly, I said, the only reason I can think of why Bev would want to marry anybody would be to make fun of what he was reading. Whenever she found a copy of *Golf Digest* on the coffee table, she'd do a minuet.

I even told Janie Ruth about my first wife, Joy Needham, who was still in Fort Worth—and still a good friend.

But I said that Joy was so long ago, and we were so young at the time, it was hard for me to consider her an official wife in the standings.

"I must be a good-humored son of a bitch," I said. "All my wives still like me."

Janie Ruth poked me on the arm, grinning.

And she said:

"You just a marryin' machine, is all you are."

She went with me, though. Janie Ruth did. Just like that. She was sort of grateful in a way. As she explained:

"Hell, I'd take off my clothes and make a movie with a donkey to get out of *this* town."

I put Janie Ruth on my arm and went everywhere, just as though I'd been drinking that whiskey which sometimes makes you invisible.

Hi, Barbara. Hi, Winnie. How you all doin'? Say, uh,

I'd like to introduce you to my niece from Fort Worth.

Well, that didn't fool anybody, of course. So when Janie Ruth and I would stumble across anyone out here who knew Beverly and knew we were still married—legally, at least—I would adopt that age-old philosophy of Mahatma Gandhi and say to myself, "Fuck it, I'm caught."

Among the first things I did with Janie Ruth was take her to Europe. That's what you're supposed to do with a free-spirited roommate, isn't it? Show off?

My excuse for Europe was the British Open. I'd been wanting to play in it some day, and it was St. Andrews' turn to be the host course. Well, there's never been a golfer who didn't want to see St. Andrews. So I figured I might as well go find out what that zoo looked like up close. It would be a history deal, if nothing else.

We stopped in London first. I decided to do it right. And I had those two old chums with me to help out—Master Charge and Visa.

I got us a suite in the Hyde Park Hotel and a limousine with a driver. I wasn't about to rent a car and try to learn how to sightsee from the wrong side of the road.

London sure was British, as Janie Ruth said.

She managed to do her share of shopping. I don't remember what she bought the most of, blonde mink coats or ashtrays.

I discovered shepherd's pie and sausage rolls, so my food case was handled.

We liked just about everything in London except the ice cube situation.

And as Janie Ruth said, "Shit, I could have a ball over here just listenin' to these people *talk*."

We arrived in St. Andrews on Sunday, which gave me three days of practice.

Janie Ruth and I stayed at the Old Course Hotel, which is right there on the "Road Hole" at St. Andrews. A par four. The 17th. There didn't used to be anything there but an old railway shed, they tell me, which you could cut across on your tee shot.

Now there's a high-rise hotel, which forces more of a dogleg. And if you try to cut across too much you're liable to hit Barbara Nicklaus or Linda Watson standing on their balconies.

I liked the golf course more than I thought I would. There isn't a tree anywhere, but I'll guarantee you those golf courses have some trouble off the fairways in the form of heather.

Heather is a mean-ass dwarf plant with dark purplish buds that holds onto your poor old golf ball like a claw. If you try to swing a club through it, you can come away with your hands ringing like a door chime. Try to hit a shot out of heather and everything just goes kind of "schoomp." The ball doesn't move. And you've got this hum in your hands.

On the night before the tournament began, I had planned something restful. For a while I went downstairs to the basement of the Old Course Hotel and fooled around with my clubs like Arnold does. Regripped my 5-iron and took some weight off my putter.

I figured Janie Ruth and I would order dinner in the room and maybe turn on the television and listen to a BBC panel discuss the dreadful condition of "North

Country poetry," or some such thing. It didn't matter to Janie Ruth what was on. She would say, "Turn on the tube and let's listen to them silly fuckers talk for a while."

What happened when I came in the room, however, was that Janie Ruth handed me this letter which had arrived for me from Joy Needham, old number one, the former Paschal High cheerleader, now a light-running whore, and the only person I've ever known who drank V.O. with Dr. Pepper.

It wasn't unusual for me to get a letter from Joy Needham occasionally. She wrote me notes to keep me up on what was happening in Fort Worth, and also, now and then, to ask if she could borrow some money.

Joy Needham represents a part of my life which is still very much with me.

We were high school sweethearts who probably never would have gotten married if she hadn't accidentally become pregnant while she was still wearing my Paschal High letter jacket. And if she hadn't had five brothers who were all capable of committing various atrocities.

Joy didn't want to be married any more than I did, and after she arranged one of the quickest abortions in the history of Fort Worth we didn't stay married much longer.

I had always felt a strong affection for Joy, even though you could say she had the morals of a three-quarter rat. She was wild, outrageous, horny, foul-mouthed, uncontrollable. All those things. But she was cute, sweet, and never boring. And maybe, looking back, it wasn't her I ever cared so much about, but all of

37

the laughter and freedom which seemed to go along with those days.

Joy's brothers were not so easily forgettable, either.

There was Waylon Needham. He was the oldest and probably the baddest. And then there were Buddy, James, Troy, and J.R.

Joy and Troy were twins and Buddy and James were twins, and J.R. was the youngest. The brothers were all about as mean and unpredictable and notorious as any group of hard-asses you could assemble.

All of the Needham brothers were built like fullbacks of varying sizes. They had crew cuts and freckles on their faces and arms, and they hardly ever smiled. One of the very large treats when we were in high school was watching the Needhams fight in the Golden Gloves. They stood straight up and held their fists out in front of them like John L. Sullivan, or somebody, and their almost-shaved heads would bob back and forth like chickens. But they would just kick the livin' dog shit out of everybody.

They usually fought in different weights, but once Buddy had to go up against Troy, and it was quite a fight until Buddy got a cut eye and Troy won on a TKO. Later, as I recall, Waylon held Troy out in the street while Buddy hit him with a roll of dimes and cut Troy's eye. So that meant the whole thing had been a draw. At least in the logic of the Needhams.

One of the charming pastimes of the Needhams was to search out some innocent guy parked with his date or girl friend at a place like the Two Country Boys Drive-In having a beer, whereupon they would terrorize him.

I was their friend as well as their football and basketball teammate, but if the Needhams were in the mood to
slap somebody around and they couldn't find a Catholic
or a Jew or a spade or somebody from another high
school, a friend was in trouble.

A Needham would approach your car, and it was easy
to determine whether a Needham was feeling ill-
tempered. If he had broken off a couple of radio aerials
or punctured any tires before he reached your car, he
was definitely ill-tempered. And then, of course, if the
Needham also happened to be wearing no shirt—just his
Levis and tennis shoes and a pair of black kid gloves—
that meant he was ready to fix himself a "prick-burger."

I think it was Waylon who described to me once what
a "prick-burger" was.

Waylon said, "You get you a sissy sumbitch who won't
fight you and you make him take his clothes off. Then
you make him hold one half of a hamburger bun on his
chest and the other half on his ass. And then you make
the sumbitch go in Burger King and ask for double
cheese."

The Needhams had a splendid way of getting somebody to climb out of his car and fight. Or at least get hit
once.

If you simply sat there next to your terrified date, or
girl friend, one of the Needhams would jerk open the car
door and piss in your lap.

I always hopped right out, pretended that I was ready
to fight, danced around for a minute, got the crap
knocked out of me, and then got up and stuck out my
hand and said:

"Sure do thank you, J.R."

There was this time that Waylon and Troy took our entire high school prisoner.

They went out and got drunk at Herb's Cafe, which was a place not far from the school where several of us hung out to drink beer and bet it up on the pinball and the puck-bowling machines. And occasionally eat a chicken-fried steak on biscuits with cream gravy.

Incidentally, in all of my worldly travels, I have rarely found anything I liked better than chicken-fried steak on biscuits with cream gravy—French fries on the side—at Herb's Cafe. A lot of times in wonderful restaurants from coast to coast where I knew I was going to spend $100 before I got out, I wished that I had eaten something as good as Herb's chicken-fried steak for $5.75.

Anyhow, Waylon and Troy got drunk at Herb's and when they went back to school they got the brilliant idea to go straight into the principal's office. Old man Firkins.

Troy pulled a knife on Old man Firkins and told him to sit still behind his desk, and not move, or he'd be going home that afternoon with an off-brand ass hole.

Waylon then went over to the table where the PA system was. And he spoke into the microphone to all of the classrooms on all three stories of the building.

I remember that Joy and I were in fifth-period study hall at the time, back there in the rear of the room, feeling around on each other, when Waylon's voice came out of the loudspeaker up in the corner of the room.

Waylon's voice said:

"Attention to ever-body concerned with Paschal High

School. Purple and white, fight, fight. They's been a military takeover here. This is your new Commander and Chief speakin'.

"Ever-body at Arlington Heights eats shit with raisins in it. That's one thing. The other thing is, so does ever-body at North Side. Except Wanda Sue Tucker."

There was a good bit of giggling from the loudspeaker and then Waylon said:

"Now I want to see all of the teachers down in the boiler room in ten minutes. We gonna find out . . . once and for all . . . which one of you has got the most poot stains on your underwear."

There was prolonged howling from the loudspeaker, which Joy and I determined to be coming from Troy.

Then Waylon's voice said:

"They's one final thing. I want to announce a new curriculum. This regime is pleased to say that we're doin' away with English, math, history, science, and social studies."

There was some more snickering over the loudspeaker and then Waylon said:

"What this means is, we will therefore have a lot more time to devote to serious things like physical education . . . football . . . polo . . . and fuckin' and suckin'."

If you think the Needhams might have been expelled for something like that, you just can't appreciate how frightened everybody was of the whole family. Besides, Waylon was the best fullback Paschal ever had. Maybe there are a few who would say that my nephew, Billy Clyde Puckett, who became a star in college and the

41

pros, was better than Waylon in high school. But I don't think anybody would suggest this to Waylon. Even me. Right now.

At any rate, the only thing old man Firkins managed to get done in the way of punishment for Waylon and Troy was make them publicly apologize to the school during an assembly.

They strolled out on the stage together, hanging their heads down, and Waylon spoke for the two of them.

Waylon said:

"Uh . . . me and Troy . . . we, uh . . . we done a bad thing the other day . . . and, uh . . . Mr. Firkins says we owe ever-body an apology . . . So, uh . . . speakin' for Troy and me . . . I just want to say that . . . uh . . . we ain't gonna make our language so public no more when we . . . uh . . . get ourselves on the outside of so much of that damned old beer. Thankee."

The band struck up the fight song and Waylon and Troy marched triumphantly off the stage, each one scratching his temple with his middle finger—a gesture which did not go unnoticed by the laughing hordes in the assembly.

It was just after we got out of high school that Waylon got his right leg amputated at the knee. It happened because the Needhams were out disturbing the peace one night by loading up water guns with black ink and stopping their car at the curb long enough to squirt people. It's sad for me to report that I was with them.

Waylon would still have two legs today if J.R. hadn't made the mistake of squirting the wrong person out on the sidewalk in front of the B-52 Lounge. Who he squirted was Bad Hair Wimberly.

Bad Hair Wimberly was a few years older than the rest of us, and he was something of a legend. He was the kind of a guy that when he walked into a bar or a pool hall everybody smiled cordially and tried to disappear.

Nobody ever questioned the fact that Bad Hair Wimberly was king of the Fort Worth street fighters. All anyone actually knew about him was that he was big, he had a psycho glaze to his eyes, and everybody said he had been to Chicago.

Waylon Needham certainly knew Bad Hair Wimberly's reputation, and Bad Hair knew Waylon's. But out of some kind of mutual respect they had avoided ever fighting each other.

When Troy pulled the car up in front of the B-52 Lounge, J.R. stuck the water gun out of the window and squirted a blob of black ink on what he thought was the back of a guy's neck, and part of his light-blue rayon sport coat. None of us looked carefully enough to see who the guy might be. But I had an awful premonition when I heard the guy yell, "Sorry motherfuckin' lice!"

We should have driven off. But Waylon said, "Let me have him. Let me have him."

I said, "Oh, shit, mother, fuck, it's Bad Hair Wimberly."

"Let's stomp his ass," said Troy. "All of us."

"That ain't fair," Waylon said. "I'll take him."

"Up fair's ass," I said. "Get this vehicle out of here."

And Bad Hair was yelling at us now.

"Waylon Needham in that fuckin' car?" Bad Hair said. "Come on, Waylon! Come on! Piss on them gnatfuckin' brothers! I want *you*, goddamn it! Kick your fuckin' teeth through the back end of your motherfuckin' . . ."

Waylon was out of the car and into Bad Hair before Bad Hair could finish.

It was the all-time Fort Worth street fight. They went at it for at least twenty minutes. I counted three clean knockdowns for Waylon and just as many for Bad Hair. Nobody won the wrestling on the pavement. The kicking was even.

The end came when Waylon took a wild swing at Bad Hair and missed. Hit a parking meter instead. He bent over for a second with his fist between his legs and said, "Geeeaaaiii, fuck!" And before he could straighten up, Bad Hair caught him with an uppercut whopper. Flipped him backwards. And while Waylon was slightly dazed, Bad Hair picked him up and threw him through the plate-glass window of Leon's Bar-B-Q.

Cut Waylon's leg so bad they had to amputate.

In the record book it says that Bad Hair Wimberly won the big fight in front of the B-52 Lounge. But did he really?

About a month later J.R. found Bad Hair shooting snooker up at Hubert's Recreation Hall. Slipped up behind him and shot him in the back of the head with a .38 while Bad Hair was trying to bank the six ball in a game of call pocket.

The police wrote the murder off as an accident. One reason was, they were delighted to be rid of Bad Hair

Wimberly. And the other thing was, it looked like J.R. had a real good chance to win the State high hurdles.

Not very long after that Waylon proved how tough he really was. He got him an artificial leg immediately and learned how to get around on it good enough to get a scholarship to North Texas State in the shot put and discus. Otherwise, he would have gone on football, of course. With two legs, I mean.

In any case, while he was getting accustomed to his artificial leg that summer he worked in his daddy's filling station. And he was there alone one afternoon when this Eldorado pulled up and two spades got out. One of them had a little old .22 pistol and they ordered Waylon to empty the cash register.

The first thing Waylon did, of course, was tell them what he thought about "niggers" in general. This one spade shot Waylon twice in the stomach, but it didn't prevent Waylon from taking the gun away from the guy, and then unstrapping his artificial leg and beating them with it until they both had a hernia and lay in a coma.

Then Waylon limped over to the telephone, the way I heard it, and called the cops and said:

"Uh, this is Waylon Needham out here on the south side at Texaco No. 8. I need some kind of ambulance for myself. And you can send a garbage truck for some shit I got layin' in the street at 4219 Hemphill."

So much for the saga of the Needham brothers right now. I've never been able to dwell on them for very long at a time without wishing I was inside an armored tank.

I used to tell all of these stories about the Needhams to Beverly, and she would plead for more intricate details.

PART 1

But when I told them to Janie Ruth she would only frown and say something like:

"I spent a lot of my better years tryin' to get away from them kind of turds."

I've often thought about the remarkable similarity between the way Janie Ruth Rimmer and Joy Needham expressed themselves. They both talked in a country accent on purpose, as many people in Fort Worth do, believing it to be entertaining and honest, almost as if clinging to a pride of ignorance was some sort of a defense against the evils of the outside world.

Which is anything non-Texan.

I thought of this again while I sat there in the hotel room in Scotland with Janie Ruth and read Joy's letter.

The letter said:

Dear Kenny:

Sure bet you're surprised to hear from Joy the Toy while you're having your tea and crumpets. I wish I could go across an ocean one of these days but I can't seem to get past Shreveport.

As you know, Kenny, I've done pretty good, off and on, in the whore-lady business, but something has happened to the trade lately and it just ain't no good any more.

I think what's happened is a recent trend among Fort Worth housewives toward neighborhood sport-fuckin'.

It's sure come at a bad time because I have an opportunity to get out of the whore-lady business right now if I had some money.

If I had $3,000 I could become a partner in Clarice Hubbard's boutique in a real nice shopping

46

mall out on 303. How are you fixed for $3,000, Kenny? Actually, I was wondering how you were fixed for $5,000 because I really need to have some work done by the tooth dentist.

I know you've always been disappointed in me, but the whore-lady business ain't that bad of a thing to do, considering that everybody in this old world is always fuckin' somebody in one way or another.

Besides, as you know, I was always a high class whore-lady, and if I hadn't been getting paid for it I would have been fuckin' a lot of guys anyhow because it always seemed like the most fun you could have.

I hate to bring this up, Kenny, but if you can't loan me the money for the boutique and the tooth dentist, I may have to resort to some blackmail.

I was talking to a good customer of mine on the newspaper not long ago, and he knows you. And we were talking about how you used to hustle everybody at Goat Hills, and this guy said he bet that a magazine like Sports Illustrated *would probably pay a lot of money for a story about how somebody on the golf tour used to be a hustler who went in the can and intentionally lost a lot of amateur tournaments one time.*

I know good and well that you throwed off the City Championship once because you were 6-up on Robbie Dee Vance in the finals with only 10 holes to play, and you lost, and you came home with a lot of money.

Anyhow, I might think about telling this to somebody if you can't loan me the money. But I know you'll give me the money if your wife—what's her name?—hasn't spent most of it for you.

Honestly, Kenny, I wouldn't need to be asking for the loan if it hadn't been for all this neighborhood sport-fuckin'.

I still look good, Kenny, despite all the troops that have marched through the Northwest Passage. Thinking about the fun times we used to have in bed and elsewhere helps me tolerate Fort Worth.

I've still got my sense of humor, thank goodness. You wouldn't believe the corner where the Two Country Boys Drive-In used to be. It's a bank building now! Who the shit wants to drink beer in a bank? Ha, ha, ho.

Stay a sweet thing now, you hear? And please make me the loan for the boutique and the tooth dentist.

Incidentally, Paschal might be really good next season. Praise to thee Paschal, purple reign. They've finally got a fast nigger.

I think they can go all the way to State.

All my love,
Joy the Toy

Janie Ruth was not especially excited about Joy's letter. She said it seemed rather personal to come from somebody so far back in the past.

She said:

"I don't see how in the hell you could have been so much fun in the sack in them days. That was before you knowed about vibrators and poppers, wasn't it?"

What happened next was unique, I believe, in the annals of marital relationships. The phone rang and it was Beverly calling from Dallas.

I thought to myself, well, this is pretty good. I wonder how one of those Bobby Joneses or Ben Hogans would handle this kind of a jackpot on the eve of a major championship? I've got a wife on the phone, a wife in a letter, and some kind of a wife in the room.

Beverly had been having a few cocktails and she had just decided to call me up in Scotland and ask me, among other things, why I had acted so rude this last time we ran into each other in public after we had separated?

For a moment, I didn't know what she was talking about.

She said I damn well did. Said it was during the Los Angeles Open and I was in the Bel Air Hotel bar with Bob Drum and some drunks from CBS and she— Beverly—had walked in with a group of people and sat across the room and then very happily noticed that I was there. Said she came over to our table, but all I did was jump up and take her aside.

Never introduced her to the Ed Sneeds, who she hadn't met. And then I hastily excused myself and left.

I said, "That was *months* ago, Bev. We were already leading separate lives. Besides, it was awkward."

She said, "I didn't know it was awkward to be polite. I was your wife, after all."

I said, "Well, I'm sorry. You were just the last person I had expected to see in the Bel Air bar. You and those terrorists you were with."

She said, "I'm afraid they were artists."

That's good, I said. We need those.

Bev said, "One of them happened to be the world's finest painter of armadillos. He will probably be to the armadillo what Russell and Remington were to the longhorn."

"Is that a good deal?" I said.

Bev said, "You obviously don't care anything at all about the armadillo, do you? The fact that the armadillo has suffered such deplorable P.R. all these years."

I said, "Bev, you're in Dallas and I'm in Scotland. Does that about wrap it up?"

She said, "Listen, Ken. The reason I called is, I was sitting here having a drink, and I was feeling kind of sentimental, and thought I would like to tell you that I never hated golf."

I lit a cigarette.

Bev said, "All I ever said, Ken, was that it disappointed me to see someone choose golf over life."

I said, "Well, it doesn't matter a lot now. But you knew golf was my business when we jacked around and got married."

"I know," she said. "I can remember gazing dimly into the future and seeing this good-looking person modeling a new line of slacks in a four-color magazine ad."

Very funny, I said.

She said, "I have been asked a number of times by friends why we were ever married, and my answer is always the same. You told me funny stories. And you didn't sell mutual funds for a living. Listen, how's Scotland? The last time I was there I saw about ninety-five places where Robert Burns was born."

Scotland was Scotland, I said.

Beverly said, "I was a bitch, Ken. That's something else I wanted to say. Most of the time, I was a bitch. But you'll have to admit it wasn't easy for me to try to adjust to your style of life."

Never took her to a bad place, I said.

"The travel was quaint," she said. "But our lives lacked quality."

I said, "Well, we didn't go to very many operas, if that's what you mean."

She said, "I was always terribly proud of you, Ken. You do what you do very well. You're lucky. Men are lucky. You've got something you love—golf—and that's great. All I ever wanted was for you to be a larger person."

I said I could be large as hell if I could win the British Open.

About then, Janie Ruth said something to me, and Beverly heard her voice.

I believe Janie Ruth said:

"You better hang up on that cunt or I'm gonna unravel ever pair of double knits you got in the closet."

Beverly inquired if that female voice she heard belonged to the chambermaid.

I said, "Bev, I know Katie Smithern has told you about Janie Ruth by now. Janie Ruth's with me. I'll probably marry her."

There was a slight pause.

Then Bev said, "This is just a crazy . . . giddy . . . stab in the dark, Ken, but does Janie Ruth have a good body?"

I said hmmmm.

Bev said, "You know, Ken, it hasn't been exactly flattering to me. Janie Ruth being with you and all. And there might even be those among your swell friends on the tour who have wondered how you could embarrass yourself like that. Have you thought lately where your dignity was? Or your character?"

I said, "Hell, Bev, I'm still trying to find me a golf swing I can rely on. I don't know where that other shit is."

We didn't say anything for a moment.

Then I said:

"What's the story on the divorce, by the way?"

Bev said, "Oh, I almost forgot. It's final. Happy fucking divorce."

Which was why she had called. To tell me.

She said, "Yep, today was officially proclaimed Mental Cruelty Day in Dallas, and I have been celebrating. I had an extra enchilada on the deluxe dinner at Casa Dominguez, and I've had several extra Scotches."

I said, well, I would celebrate, too, but with a lot less ice in my glass.

She said, "Listen, Ken. Seriously. I'd like to see you when you come back from Scotland. You've still got a few things here at the apartment. Would the hard-hitting Janie Ruth mind?"

Probably, I said. But I would try. And then I told Bev about getting the letter from Joy Needham, and that I had just been reading it when the phone rang. So, essentially, I said, I was surrounded by women.

"We all need to be there running in and out of a lot of doors," Bev said.

I mentioned to Bev what had been in Joy's letter.

Bev said, "Hey, you should be so lucky that *Sports Illustrated* would print a story like that. It would certainly make you more colorful to the crowds."

She said, "Incidentally, now that we're divorced, I can say this. I look terrific."

I said, well, she never had been an unplayable lie.

Then Bev said, "You know what would be spiffy? You marry Janie Ruth, and I'll be the mistress. See how she feels about that."

I said hmmmm.

Bev said, "Have I ever told you that I'm truly sorry it didn't work?"

I said I knew she was.

"It was just too complicated," I said. "We're both better off. We really are."

"Now then," she said. "We'd better hang up, but I want to leave you with an important thought. You can dwell on it, not just in Scotland, but throughout your career as you plod steadfastly over all of the botanical venues of your profession. Just remember it came from me."

"Okay," I said.

And Beverly said, "Ballantyne cashmeres fit you much better than Pringles."

Now of course I didn't get to devote the rest of the evening to thinking about St. Andrews, and all the historical features of it that I'd be playing golf on the next day. Things like Hell Bunker, The Valley of Sin, the Principal's Nose, the Road Hole, and The Loop.

Naw, I had to spend the rest of the night trying to

convince Janie Ruth that I wasn't still in love with either one of my two ex-wives.

Janie Ruth said at one point, "The only reason you want me around is because you're some kind of a degenerate tit freak."

I played well in Scotland, I thought, considering the wind and the rain and the fact that I could never stop laughing at my caddy.

My caddy was about ninety-eight years old, he wore an overcoat and a gangster's cap, and he kept about half of a damp cigarette in his mouth at all times.

I never managed to put a real low number up on the board at St. Andrews, and my caddy said it was because I couldn't "cane the loop."

"Aye, Lad," he would say. "If you can na' cane the loop, you can na' play the Old Course."

The Loop at St. Andrews is a portion of the course—three holes, the 9th, 10th and 11th—where it bends around away from the sea and starts back toward the big gray stone building which serves as both the clubhouse and the headquarters for the Royal & Ancient.

To "cane the loop," which means to flog it, you're supposed to play those holes in two under par.

I caned a lot of Dover sole, but I never caned the loop.

From the first day I knew my caddy was going to be an experience. After I hit my first tee ball in practice on No. 1, I asked him what club I should use to get over Swilken's Burn, the little brook which edges up against the green.

He handed me the 8-iron.

"Soft eight or hard eight?" I asked.

He said:

"Just the true value of the club, Lad."

Later on I hit what I thought was a good shot into the 11th, but it caught a hard spot and kicked to the back of the green.

"Right on line," I said.

"Aye, Lad," he said. "That's half the game, isn't it?"

And then on the 18th once, above The Valley of Sin, I had this tricky putt that I was trying to read.

"Is this thing going left or right?" I said.

And he said:

"Aye, it's a bit of a lottery, Lad."

I think I wound up tied for seventh when the tournament was over, and any time you finish among the best ten in golf it means you could have won if God hadn't been slightly pissed off at you.

Overall, the trip to England and Scotland was fairly educational. Once you get used to your coffee tasting like stewed dirt, you can settle down and enjoy the atmosphere.

As Janie Ruth so graphically put it one day at the Tower of London:

"How in the hell can the Alamo and Goliad and Sam Houston go up against all this king-and-queen shit?"

The French Open followed Scotland and I'd made arrangements to play in it. The tournaments in Europe will offer an American pro almost anything to get him there. I settled for a free suite at the Hotel du Palais in Biarritz, France, where the tournament was.

We went through Paris for a day so Janie Ruth could look for Ava Gardner. Then we whipped on down to

PART 1

Biarritz and a French Open I knew I wouldn't take too seriously. The prize money didn't amount to much more than a casual afternoon at Goat Hills in the old days.

There weren't any crowds, the competitors were mostly Spaniards and Italians, and the golf course—La Nivelle, I think they called it—looked like it hadn't been mowed since Napoleon's last visit.

None of that mattered. The hotel was worth the trip. It was huge and it hung out above the beach and the ocean. Off our balcony we could look down on all kinds of skin. Whoever said the French didn't have any tits must not have been to Biarritz.

We decided, however, that the best thing you could say for the French was that they know how to cook. Especially when they go with their omelettes, soups, and shoestrings.

If you fight your way through all of those s'il vous fuckin' plaits and manage to get something ordered you like, you've got yourself a taste treat. You just want to make sure a Frenchman doesn't try to cold-jump you with a mushroom or a snail or an off-brand vegetable.

Dining in France reminded me of all the debates I used to have with Beverly about food. She said that all those years I ate at Herb's Cafe had insured the fact that I would never like anything which wasn't brown and white, and usually fried.

I used to insist this wasn't true. "I like pinto beans," I said. "And they're maroon."

Bev relentlessly tried to spring gourmet dishes on me. If it wasn't something puréed, it would be oddly shaped or a peculiar color like green, yellow, or orange. Sometimes it would be something that started with a "z."

56

One night in Dallas I was joking around with Bev and I originated "the first annual World Vegetable Match Play Classic."

I drew up the pairings and the brackets and wrote in the winners and Scotch-taped it on the kitchen wall by the pad where she made out her grocery list.

In the first round Arnold Squash defeated Gary Spinach, Lord Byron Broccoli whipped Slammin' Sam Turnips, Big Jack, the Golden Okra, dusted off Bantam Ben Cauliflower, and Lee Eggplant beat Bobby Carrots.

In the second round Arnold Squash knocked off Bryon Broccoli, and Jack Okra stomped Lee Eggplant.

And then in the finals Jack Okra went into sudden death against Arnold Squash, and nosed him out on the 22nd hole.

"Was there a big gallery at this tournament?" Bev asked.

"Yeah," I said. "A lot of beets and cabbage."

She looked at the results and said:

"And this insinuates that okra is the killer, right?"

I said, "Okra's good for two vomits almost any day or night. The only thing I know of that can put okra away is tripe."

Bev said, "I don't happen to like it either. But tripe and onions is considered a delicacy by some people. In any case, tripe is hardly a vegetable."

I said, "It fuckin' well ought to be."

The French Open, to my mind, was highlighted by the ability of some barefooted caddies to tee up a ball in the rough with their big toes. The Spanish players all had these barefooted caddies, who also carried along in their pockets a good supply of Dunlop 65s they could slide down their trouser legs in case a Spanish pro might not be able to find his tee shots over in the woods.

I believe I finished tied for fourth with some kind of an Englishman, behind three Spanish cheaters.

The whole thing reminded me of Goat Hills and people like Spec Reynolds and T. Lou (Tiny) Fawver and Hope-I-Do Collins.

For unknowns, there were some people at Goat Hills who could dead solid play golf, and they had you keeping your wits about you because in most games there was a new bet on every backswing.

If you couldn't shoot the lights out at Goat Hills, then you needed either Pretty Boy Floyd or John Dillinger for a partner. Otherwise, they shipped your body home.

If I ever play on the Continent again, I guarantee you I'll have a barefooted caddy with a nimble big toe.

Our return from Europe was slightly picturesque. Primarily because of a heart-stirring confrontation between Janie Ruth and Beverly in the old Dallas airport, Love Field.

We had flown practically nonstop from Biarritz to Paris to New York to Dallas, and I certainly didn't expect anyone to be waiting for us in the Love Field lobby but the tall granite statue of the Texas Ranger.

There was Beverly, however.

She'd found out when I was arriving in Dallas from Katie Smithern. I'd phoned Katie to ask her if she minded putting us up for a few days while we recovered from Europe. Katie never minded my drop-ins. Ever since I'd moved out on Bev my temporary home had been Donny and Katie's house.

I intended to get another apartment of my own, of course, if I was ever in town long enough. Meanwhile, I was always welcome in the Smithern mansion. With or without a companion, who would not be Beverly.

Katie never made any judgments. She just smiled a lot, and shelled peas, and cleaned. Donny didn't allow Katie many opinions.

She was Beverly's friend, though, and I couldn't blame her for telling Bev when I was coming.

So there I was, anyhow, trapped in the airport. It was an obvious case of "Thanks again, God."

I thought I would try a little humor on Bev at first. I smiled and stuck out my hand like one of those Madison Avenue fellows and said:

"Hi. I'm Jerry Danford. Network sales."

And then I took Janie Ruth by the arm and said to Beverly:

"I'd like for you to meet the greatest putter I've ever come across. This is Ben Crenshaw."

I'm not sure why I felt so guilty. Beverly and I were divorced now. But I couldn't help thinking about Donny Smithern's idea of how to handle a public crisis of this nature.

Donny always said, "Even if they have an eyewitness, don't plead guilty. There's no recourse from guilty except mercy. And what woman ever had any mercy?"

Donny liked to say:

"The few times I've had something illegal on my arm and gotten caught, I've simply introduced myself as Norman Huddleston, a mining engineer from Santiago. Who some people claim is a dead look-alike for Donny Smithern, the golfer."

59

In any event, Beverly just stood there looking at us rather coldly.

Then suddenly Janie Ruth went into this monologue. She said:

"Beverly, you can think whatever you want to about me and Kenny. But you don't have no stamp on him no more. You can go ahead and practice hate if you want to, and stand there lookin' like you wouldn't give the road to a bear. But Kenny and me are in love, and God don't frown on love. Besides, Kenny's a man, is all he is. And I don't think it ought to be held against him because he likes air travel and pretty girls and happiness."

The only way I can describe the expression on Bev's face while Janie Ruth was talking would be to say that it was bewildered-curious.

And when Janie Ruth had finished, Bev only looked at first one and then the other of us, and back again, and then folded her arms and said slowly to me:

"Un . . . fucking . . . believable."

I asked Bev if she had taken up the habit of hanging around airports in the afternoon. Or had she come out there to try and embarrass me?

She said, "I didn't want to miss you, and I figured you might not call while you were here."

Janie Ruth said, "He won't."

Sort of ignoring Janie Ruth's presence, Bev said:

"I'd really like for you to come by for a drink. You can pick up the rest of your things, and we can chat. We're at least pals, right?"

I said, well, I didn't know whether I could or not. One thing I intended to do was sleep for a couple of days.

And I had to think about whether I was going to live in Dallas or somewhere else.

I put my arm around Janie Ruth's waist, as if to assure everybody of who I was with.

Bev said, "You know, Ken, I just can't envision you hanging out the clothes to dry in your marvelous little mobile home community while what's-her-name here sits on the steps of the trailer dyeing the eggs for Easter."

Janie Ruth squinted at Bev and said:

"Is that remark as smart-alec as I think it is?"

Bev kept looking at me and said:

"I thought you'd been around enough country clubs by now to recognize class."

Then Janie Ruth looked at me and said, "What's that shit mean about Easter eggs?"

Everybody decided to smoke a cigarette.

Bev then turned to my companion and said:

"Do you travel frequently with other people's husbands?"

And Janie Ruth said, "Only them that take me first cabin. What are *you* supposed to be? Some kind of a *moralist?*"

Beverly looked at me and laughed.

Janie Ruth said, "Kenny, I think we ought to go get the luggage."

That didn't seem like a bad idea, I said.

Beverly said, "Ken, I really would like to see you privately."

"I can't say for sure," I said.

"Well, I can," said Janie Ruth.

I said, "Let me give you a call in a day or two, Bev."

Janie Ruth said, "You're gonna do *what*?"

And kicked me in the shin with the heel of her boot.

I told Janie Ruth to calm down. What would it matter for me to visit with Bev? I had to pick up the rest of my stuff, anyhow.

"Do you *love* me?" Janie Ruth said.

I said, "Of course."

Bev said, "Of course not."

"Well, do you?" said Janie Ruth.

I said, "That's got nothing to do with any of this."

I hugged on Janie Ruth.

And I said, "You know how I feel about you. But Bev and I aren't mortal enemies. She just wants to visit with me."

It was about then that I realized we had a gallery in the lobby of the airport. A few feet away were a photographer and a guy with a pad and pencil.

I asked what they wanted. They said they were from *The Dallas Morning News* and they had been sent out to get my picture and to interview me about my experiences in Europe.

The photographer said, "Kenny, why don't you and your wife and sister move in there close. I'll get a couple of shots."

Beverly grinned at Janie Ruth and said:

"Which one do you want to be, pet?"

I took the newspaper guys aside and asked them if they would mind if we did the interview and the pictures over at Donny Smithern's house later on? They said fine.

When I returned to my ladies, Janie Ruth was saying:

"You're supposed to be rich. You could buy all kinds of men. Why do you want Kenny?"

Beverly said, "I don't happen to *want* Ken, my dear. I've been there."

I cleared my throat.

Bev went on, "I enjoy talking to him, however. He comes close to being my best buddy."

I looked at Bev sort of curiously.

She said to me, "Never knew that, did you?"

Then Janie Ruth said, "God damn it, Kenny, I'm wore out from this trip. And I want to get out of this airport *right now.*"

"We've really got to go," I said to Bev. "I'll call you in a day or two."

"Bull . . . *shit*," Janie Ruth said. "You'll call for help first."

Janie Ruth and I started slowly toward the baggage claim area. I glanced back subtly over the old shoulder and saw Bev going past the statue of the Texas Ranger.

She was saluting.

On the subject of more recent history, such as what was going on at Heavenly Pines, I can report firsthand that when you find yourself among the National Open leaders you take on a celebrity status you hadn't otherwise known.

That Thursday night Janie Ruth and I went out to dinner with Donny and Katie. And while we were out there in public I was asked to sign as many autographs as Donny, which was a first for Kenny Puckett.

We'd driven through the North Carolina forests and sandhills and down the main highway toward Raleigh to a Polynesian restaurant near a theme park, drag strip, car wash, drive-in movie, go-cart track and Astroturf poly-snow ski slope.

Janie Ruth referred to the restaurant as "Trapper Vic's."

Although dozens of customers were waiting for tables, the four of us got ushered past everybody and seated. The owner was at the door greeting people and he recognized me from the six o'clock news even before he saw Donny.

"Good thing I played good," I said.

"I could have handled it," Donny said.

All through dinner we kept getting menus passed over to us that we were supposed to sign. I was accustomed to watching Donny do this sort of thing. But it rarely happened to me.

Occasionally Donny would sometimes remember to tell the fan that I was a good player, too. Say hello to Kenny Puckett. The fan would feel embarrassed for himself *and* me. And he would say, "Oh, yeah. Sure. Puckett. Yeah, uh . . . put your name right here. What'd you shoot today, anyway?"

But it was different that Thursday night.

A typical scene:

"Nice round, Kenny," says a man going past our table and slapping me on the Navy-blue blazer. "Keep it up."

Then he balances the budget with Donny.

"You, too, Smithern," he says. "Real good round. Certainly was. Fine. Good to see you boys."

Katie smiles sweetly and says, "Everyone means well. They really do."

Donny hangs in there with the sliced pork.

"Fuck 'em," he says.

Janie Ruth laughs.

And I think to myself what an incredible game it is. One stroke out of eighteen long, tough holes, and four and a half hours on the golf course. One silly shot. Maybe a three-foot putt which dropped for me, and didn't drop for somebody else. The thin, subtle, stupid, intangible difference between a 71 and a 72.

Before we left the restaurant the owner sat with us for a drink and some golf tips.

"Take it back low and slow," I said. "Stay behind the ball and keep your left side firm."

"Cheat," said Donny, yawning.

Janie Ruth wanted to compliment the owner on our dinner.

She said, "I don't know who you got back there in your kitchen, but everything was real good. By god, when they ain't foolin' around with wars and dope traffic, them slants do pretty good on the cuisine."

Back in the bedroom of our suite in a place called the Heavenly Marriott South, I tried to take a quick swipe at Janie Ruth.

But she said, "I ain't up to it, Hon. Guess I had too many of them shrimp puffs and crab fingers."

She was very good at excuses by then.

"It's just as well," I said, rolling over. "I'm worn out my own self. And I know you don't enjoy laboring over something that's soft as one of those Pillsbury refrigerated biscuits you shake out of a can."

Part 2

Problems for Society

Three

*F*RIDAY WAS THE DAY I started to get an idea of what the publicity heat is really like. The kind that a Jack Nicklaus or a Lee Trevino or a Tom Watson—even a Donny Smithern—has to live with constantly.

The only time a big name is safe is when he's inside the ropes playing his round. The rest of the time he's either talking to the press, or on camera, or trying to find the back door of the clubhouse so he can escape from nine thousand kids.

What I did was, I went out there Friday at Heavenly Pines and shot me a young 69. When you added it to my opening 71 it gave me a 36-hole total of 140—even par—and this was somehow good enough when the day ended that your poor old Kenny Puckett was all alone as the National Open leader.

Donny played good, too, and he rang up a 69 himself, so he was only one stroke back at 141. He finished just a few minutes behind me so it worked out that we wound up going into the press tent together.

It was a fairly interesting session with the writers. Donny and I sat up there on the platform behind the microphone together and needled each other pretty good.

Donny played his part well as the established star, and I just kept on acting like the fellow who might get arrested any day for impersonating a golfer.

When a couple of touring pros have an audience they can't resist lapsing into what you call your repartee.

At one point during the interview Donny said, "What'd you hit to the seventh, pard?"

I said, "Aw, I just kind of scraped a 5-iron up there."

"A *five-iron*," Donny said. "Man, I could hit balls all day and I couldn't get there with less than a three."

Then he turned to the writers and said:

"Think we'd better run a Dun & Bradstreet on Kenny's bag. He could get an IRS audit for that kind of loft."

The press got the joke. Most people who're golfwise know that a touring pro's clubs are not exactly like the ones that are sold to the public. Donny once carried a whole sack of 2-irons.

I said to Donny, "What'd you make on twelve?"

"Routine par," he said.

"A *par*?" I said. "I looked back and saw you so deep in the rough off the tee, I thought you were a natural-food addict lookin' for your lunch."

Donny grinned out at the writers.

"You couldn't have made par," I said, "without a pencil."

And Donny said, "I parred it. Driver . . . wedge . . . three-iron . . . and holed it from the bunker. That adds up to four, doesn't it?"

I said, "Boy, that's sure good news. I blew it from six feet there for a birdie."

Donny said, "Those two fours look just alike on the old scorecard, though, don't they?"

A writer asked both of us what we thought our chances of winning were over the next two days.

Donny said, "Ask us that Sunday night."

And he laughed. Heh, heh.

I said, "Well, I think you've got to say Donny has the best chance right now. He's only one shot back of me, and he's won two major championships. He knows what it's like to come down the stretch in one of these things. I don't."

Donny said, "A lot of people are still in it. It's not just us."

From the platform you could see the leaderboard in the tent which keeps the press up-to-date. It was fun to observe my name on top. But there *were* a few other gunners among the top ten that you couldn't overlook.

Through the first two rounds the board read:

K. Puckett. . . . . .71-69—140
D. Smithern . . . . .72-69—141
L. Wadkins. . . . . .71-72—143
H. Irwin . . . . .71-73—144
J. Nicklaus . . . . .75-70—145

PART 2

I said to the writers, "There's Nicklaus, for example, only five strokes back. I wouldn't feel safe from Jack if he was in a wheelchair."

Another writer said, "But if it came down to Sunday and the two of you were still first and second in the tournament, you'd be paired together. How would either of you feel about that?"

Donny said, "Hell, that'd be great! It's always better to get paired with a friend. You can put each other at ease."

The writer said, "And the Open wouldn't have any effect on your friendship?"

Donny grew humble. And he said slowly:

"Believe me . . . There's nobody I'd rather see win the tournament than Kenny, if I'm not going to. He's a fine player. He deserves to win a major championship. Remember this. The pro's real enemy is the golf course. I'm sure Kenny feels that if he can't win, he'd like to see me do it. Right, pard?"

I smiled and said, "Naw, I'd rather see Nicklaus win again. We've got to do all we can for the oppressed minorities in this country."

Donny laughed along with the tent. Then he said to the writers:

"He's not bad, is he? I've been coaching him some on how to handle you guys."

When we left the press tent Donny went to practice
and I was invited up to the clubhouse by some network-
TV guys and a couple of people from *Sports Illustrated*
who said they wanted to "get to know me better" over
some cocktails. I was flattered they wanted to visit with
me because they normally don't fool around with anybody other than Nicklaus or Trevino or Arnold, or at the
least a Donny Smithern. Certainly not with the POWs.

It's something of a convenience to sit around with
those big-time New York types like the TV and magazine
folks. The booze service is good. And strangers don't in-
trude on the table as much because they think you're
involved in something important.

I didn't kid myself that I had overnight become one of
the folklore heroes of golf. I knew they only wanted to
get familiar with me in case I accidentally pulled a Jack
Fleck or an Orville Moody and won the damn tournament. They wanted to be "protected" in other words
against the catastrophe of this thing becoming a "Kenny
Puckett Open."

I kidded them about this.

I told them I was a mediocre student of golf history
and I knew what could happen to guys who started
thinking *too soon* about winning something.

Told them the Dick Metz story. How it was that back
in 1938 at Cherry Hills it looked like Dick Metz was so
far ahead in the National Open that only the highway
patrol could catch him. How with only eighteen holes to
go this Hollywood contract had been offered to him for a
million dollars—if he won. And how he promptly went
out and shot himself a light-running 79, and blew it.

For a while on the tour in those days, I said, when a

man hit a real bad shot, he would say, "I done Dick Metz'd it."

I said I remembered the story of Hogan at Olympic in '55. How he walked off the 72nd hole, convinced he had won his fifth Open. How he went over to Joe Dey, who was the head of the USGA then, and handed him the golf ball he'd putted out with on the final green, and said, "Here, Joe. This is for Golf House." The museum.

And how an hour later here came this fellow named Jack Fleck, out of nowhere, who had lapsed into what everybody refers to as an "Open coma." Fleck not only tied Hogan, he stayed in the "coma" and beat him in the playoff.

And then, of course, I said I didn't want to be critical of *Sports Illustrated* because I usually read everything in it, including those stories about paddle tennis, beagles, and monopoly championships. But I knew how the magazine had probably "jinxed" Arnold out of at least two more Opens.

The one at Brookline he blew to Julius Boros, and the one in San Francisco he blew to Billy Casper. It was common knowledge on the tour, I said, that *Sports Illustrated* had convinced Arnold he was a dead solid lock to win, and talked him into wearing a red sweater in the final round both times. For photographic reasons. Red shows up better on a magazine cover than anything else.

Truest thing I ever heard about the pressure of the National Open, I said, came from Cary Middlecoff.

"Nobody wins the Open," he said. "It wins you."

Which means that more people lose a tournament than win it. And you can check the history books. Nobody ever made a putt on the last green—a long one, or

74

even medium-sized—to win the Open. The winner's always the guy who lost it the least.

If you stop to think about it, I said, a golfer's got more enemies than any other athlete. He's normally got all the other guys to beat, all fourteen of his clubs in the bag, eighteen different holes, grass, trees, sand, water, wind—and most of all, himself.

Somebody asked me if I'd started to feel the pressure yet at Heavenly Pines.

"Not yet," I said. "So far I've just been sneaking around out there in my quiet old blues and grays trying to get in shape to win a little money this week."

Then I said, "Maybe if I'm still in it by Sunday afternoon I'll start thinking about the immortality. I know Nicklaus says it's tougher to play against the record book than the pocketbook. I might discover that's true. But I know this. Where I come from, there was pretty good pressure when you were playing some bandits named Spec Reynolds and T. Lou (Tiny) Fawver and Hope-I-Do Collins for $25 each—and you didn't have but $10 on you."

I think if you've ever been a gambler you don't have much regard for money, and you're amused at people who do. I was hoping this attitude would help me in the Open. A lot of pros in my position would already be thinking about the $130,000 check for winning, and they'd choke quicker on that than they would on their name in a history book.

Money has never meant much to me except when I needed it to spend. I mean, I can't believe all the rich fuckers in this world who break into a sweat because they might have to touch the principal.

The last thing it would ever occur to me to do would be to accumulate so much money that I would leave a hunk of it sitting around when I ran out of air to breathe.

The only time in my life I ever tried to save anything was when I wanted to come out here. It took me over four years to stack up that $15,000 I had. It all came from the gambling games at Goat Hills and betting on Southwest Conference football.

During part of this period I was near the end of my poetic marriage to Joy Needham. Joy could destroy money as good as me, so I took to hiding it now and then, knowing that her idea of being a good homemaker was seeing to it that we had "his and her" T-birds.

Among my various hiding places were my golf bag, the *World Almanac*, and envelopes which looked as if they came from insurance companies, my theory being that Joy would never open an envelope that appeared to contain anything complicated.

The only money she ever discovered—about $600— was one time when she was thumbing through the *World Almanac* trying to look up a cure for gonorrhea.

She said I had been holding out on her with the money. I said, well, that was pretty good. She'd come up with the clap, but I was the one holding out.

She said, "I'm real sorry, Baby. I must have contracted it from one of those dirty glasses you drink out of at Herb's."

Can't get it that way, I pointed out.

"Says who?" she said.

Aw, all them doctors, I said.

She said, "Well, that's not right. You can get it from silverware and pillows and pay toilets and everywhere."

I laughed. Said it didn't much matter. I didn't care to catch it.

She said, "Baby, I don't think you've caught it from me unless you took a bite of beans off my plate the other night at Joe's Mexican joint."

I said, "Joy, there's no way you can get the clap unless you go to the Heart O'Texas Motel with Roy Kennerdine or Billy Bob Simpson or any of those other off-brand, drop-case guys you hang around with in the afternoons."

She looked hurt.

"They're just *guys* like you," she said. "They just happen to enjoy dancing and drinking instead of playing golf."

"There's another difference," I said. "I don't normally have the clap."

"I didn't get it from Roy, anyhow," she said. "I got it from a washbasin or a bed sheet or a coffee cup, or somewhere."

No way, I said.

She said, "That's what *you* say. You probably read that in *Time* magazine, or something."

I said, "God damn it, you can't get the clap except by fuckin' somebody."

She got tears in her eyes.

And I said, "It's nothing a little penicillin can't handle. I just wish you had some other hobbies."

Joy said, "I don't want to be bad, Baby. I'm just weak,

I guess. I know there must be more to life than drinkin'
and fuckin' and havin' fun. But I can't find out what it
is, other than going to the picture show."

She said, "I got all drunked-up on that V.O. and Dr.
Pepper the other afternoon while you were out at the
Abilene Invitation. And Roy gave me a marijuana cigarette and showed me some pictures from Sweden that
made me horny. And besides that, he gave me a present."

I asked what kind of present.

"I don't know yet," she said. "He gave me $25 to buy
myself something with."

I explained to Joy that she might as well consider herself a whore–lady if she intended to accept cash.

"Well, I didn't want to fuck him for zip," she said. "I
don't really like Roy Kennerdine. Do you?"

I said, "Joy, you're one of the best-looking girls in
town. But if you keep fooling around like this you're going to wind up a pure tramp."

She said, "Well, anything would be better than hanging around a bunch of *golf* tournaments."

"You could get a decent job," I said.

She said, "Everybody says I could get rich if I was a
high-type whore–lady. They might be right. I don't
know why girls give it away. We've got all the damn
pussy in the world cornered."

Well, that was certainly true, I said. And after all,
when you stopped to think about it, it was only a moral
question.

"What is?" she said.

I grinned and kissed her on the forehead.

She dabbed at her eyes with a Kleenex.

And she said, "I just wish everybody would relax and have fun and leave everybody else alone. Then there wouldn't be any problems."

We sat there for a moment.

Then she said, "I don't know what kind of a job I could get. I don't know how to be anything but a movie star."

Thinking about money reminds me of a wonderful get-rich scheme that two of Joy's brothers came up with when we were in high school.

Waylon and Troy Needham decided one afternoon that they would go into the kitchen-appliance business. And they would get their appliances from other people's kitchens.

The idea occurred to them when several of us happened to drop by a sorority meeting one day at Sandra Solomon's house. It was sort of a fad in our day for your football and basketball heroes to wander in on sorority meetings.

We would give the girls ample time to conduct their sorority business, which generally consisted of the older girls torturing the pledges into describing their sexual escapades in intimate detail.

Finally the heroes would arrive in their letter jackets to eat all of the food in the house, raise hell, and get the older girls to assign pledges to fuck us.

It was always a pleasure to go to Sandra Solomon's house because the Solomons were rich and they kept plenty of food in their refrigerator. Sandra was also popular because she won our traditional blue ribbon for "best in tits."

Troy Needham had dated Sandra Solomon until he heard she was some kind of a Jew.

When they broke up I said to Troy I thought he knew she was Jewish. Her name was Solomon.

"Shit, I just thought it was one of them fuckin' old Bible names," he said.

Anyhow, Waylon and Troy walked out of Sandra's house that day with an electric can opener, a blender, and a mixer. Took them over to Winslett's Shop 'N Swap and sold them for $40.

It didn't take long for the Needhams to figure out that if they could bring in bigger and better appliances, there would be more money in it. So they took to putting on grease-repellent uniforms to look like repairmen. They would borrow their daddy's pickup truck and go into houses where it appeared nobody was home. And carry out an appliance.

Unfortunately for the poor old Solomons the Needhams went too far one day.

Waylon, Troy, and I had spent most of the afternoon drinking beer at Herb's Cafe when we decided we'd drive over to Sandra's house to get something to eat, maybe play some records, and look at her tits.

We did that. We sat around in the living room for a while with Sandra and talked dirty. Sandra's mother came in and fixed us two or three sandwiches. I guess I didn't realize how drunk Waylon and Troy were.

Next thing I knew I heard Waylon's voice coming from the kitchen. He was saying, "I'm afraid we gonna have to confiscate this refrigerator. You got some Jew food in here, and we're with the Gestapo."

Sandra and I went in the kitchen. There were Waylon and Troy trying to move the refrigerator out from the wall.

Mrs. Solomon said, "Come on, boys. The joke's over."

Waylon picked her up by the neck and said:

"Don't you know you ain't supposed to fuck with Nazis?"

I said, "Hey, Waylon, hold on, man."

Troy was struggling with the refrigerator, and he said to me, "I bet we can sell this thing for $80 or $90."

Sandra said, "Yawl must be on dope."

Mrs. Solomon said, "You boys can just get out of here *right now* or I'll call the *police.*"

Sandra said, "Yawl aren't funny, *Waylon.*"

Waylon and Troy looked at each other in their evil way.

"Let's have a party," said Waylon.

Waylon grabbed Mrs. Solomon's arm and twisted it until tears came in her eyes. He pulled her across the floor and locked her in a linen closet.

Sandra looked at me for help. I was just standing there, bewildered. She made a move for something— anything—she might be able to pick up and swing at them with.

But Troy put a switchblade in her ribs.

"Troy!" Sandra said. "This is *me! Sandra!*"

He said, "That's right. And there's old Waylon over there. And this here is Kenny. And I'm about half drunk."

Mrs. Solomon was beating on the closet door and screaming.

"You fuckin' guys have gone crazy," I said.

Waylon said, "You don't have to go to the party if you don't want to, Kenny. But I bet you'd have fun."

"Yawl better get *out* of here," Sandra said.

I said that wasn't a bad idea.

Troy said, "Waylon, we can't move this damned old refrigerator. It's too fuckin' heavy."

"Pisses me off is what it does," Waylon said.

With that, Waylon took a butcher knife out of a drawer and went toward the living room. Troy dragged Sandra along behind him. Waylon then began carving swastikas on all of the paintings.

Troy threw Sandra down on the couch.

"God damn it, Waylon," I said. "Those things might be worth thousands of dollars. Let up, man."

Waylon said, "You want to get your ass kicked, Kenny? Who you for? Jews or white people?"

Sandra was crying and shaking. Troy had ripped her sweater off, over her head, and pulled her skirt down around her ankles.

He had unbuttoned his Levi's and reeled out his joint. He had forced her to take hold of it.

"What the hell are you guys gonna do?" I said. "Just kill everybody? Is that it?"

Waylon said, "Let's see them tits, Sandra." And he went over to Troy and Sandra on the couch. He tore off her brassiere. He jerked her panties down.

I said, "You son of a bitches can go to jail forever for this."

Waylon said, "Naw we can't. Can we, Sandra? Ain't nobody gonna tell the police nothin' because if they do, we got three more brothers and they'd kill you. Ain't that right, Sandra?"

Sandra had her eyes closed and she was gritting her teeth.

"You ain't gonna kill *me*," I said. "Because if you did, Paschal wouldn't have a goddamn quarterback. Now let's get out of here before you fuckers do anything else you're gonna regret."

Waylon thought about the quarterback situation.

"I wanted to jackoff on them tits," he said.

"This bullshit's over," I said. "Come on, Troy. Put that damn knife away. Sandra, get your clothes on. It's gonna be okay."

Sandra began struggling back into her skirt and sweater, sobbing. I told her to wait until we were gone before she let her mother out of the closet.

I had to make the concession of allowing Troy to shit on the living room carpet before I could get them out of there.

The poor Solomons were in such shock they really didn't tell the police. Mr. Solomon sold his jewelry business immediately, and I think they moved to San Jose. The Needhams' get-rich scheme was finally brought to a proper ending by their own kind. Their daddy. One day old man Needham accidentally caught them trying to steal the gas stove out of their own home.

Old man Needham went blind crazy when he saw what Waylon and Troy were doing.

He knocked out several of their teeth, and when they

were on the ground he kicked them in the ribs and the nuts. They refused to defend themselves because they honored their daddy.

Next thing old man Needham did was make Waylon and Troy stand there in the front yard and take turns slugging each other in the face. When they were finally so tired and bleeding that all they could do was sit down under the mimosa tree, old man Needham made them each drink a large jar of raw eggs, Milk of Magnesia, and piss. And when they threw up, he rubbed their faces in it.

Waylon remembered that their daddy was cussing every minute.

The last thing he did was take all of their Paschal High letter jackets and letter sweaters and throw them in a pile in the yard and set fire to them. Said they'd disgraced the purple "P."

We all secretly felt that this had been well-deserved punishment for Waylon and Troy. Only it didn't do anything but make them meaner.

Actually, the Needhams didn't always do things that were criminal and malicious. A lot of their mischief was meant to be funny, a sort of relief from the boredom of growing up in Fort Worth.

Among several of the things the Needhams despised were Catholics, although they never did anything extremely harmful to a Catholic. Other than yank a cross or a medal from around his neck on a basketball court— or beat the crap out of him after the game.

As Waylon once said, "They's an outside chance that God's a Catholic instead of a fuckin' Baptist."

What they did enjoy, however, was a good joke on a Catholic.

One of their favorite things to do was dress up like nuns and priests, and stagger around on the sidewalk waving whiskey bottles, just as people would be exiting from a movie theater.

One night a kindly gentleman went over to Troy, who was disguised as a nun outside of the Ridglea Theater. He took Troy's arm and said:

"Excuse me, Sister, but can I be of some assistance?"

In a high-pitched voice, Troy said:

"You surely can. I been cooped up out there at Our Lady of Victory on the south side, and I'm achin' to get hold of a big old warm prick."

When the man walked away in disgust, the Needhams all collapsed on the sidewalk, giggling, and chugalugged their whiskey.

They put on a marvelous act in their costumes. Buddy, James, and Troy were the nuns, and Waylon and J.R. were the priests.

After drinking and cussing and hollering at people, they started to paw around on one another, as if the priests were trying to make out with the nuns.

Waylon once yelled to the crowd:

"If any of you see that goofy little wop over in Rome who wears that baseball cap without no bill on it, tell him pussy's done ruint my mind."

Somebody finally called the police. But when the squad car pulled up the Needhams revealed their true identities and the cops began to laugh.

One of the cops said, "Shit, when we got the call I told

PART 2

old R.T. here, I bet it's them fuckin' Needhams. How's your momma 'n them, Waylon?"

I'm quite certain the Needhams felt the best joke they ever played on anybody was on Joy and I when we were struck with the urgency to get married.

The day before our moving ceremony in a non-air-conditioned room of the county courthouse, the Needhams drove out to Goat Hills and kidnapped me. I was sitting in the locker room playing gin with Spec Reynolds when I noticed I was being carried out the door.

Took me downtown, is basically what they did, to a room in the Dixon Hotel where they tied me down on a bed, naked.

Waylon then called in an overweight, orange-haired whore lady and gave her $20 to perform some intriguing surgery on me.

First, she shaved off all of my poor old pubic hair. Then she painted my joint purple—for Paschal High, of course.

"Mem-o-ries ever, in our hearts remain," Waylon sang.

Last, the Needhams got the whore–lady to peroxide the hair on my head from dark brown to off-yellow.

"He looks sort of pretty," the whore–lady said, admiring her work. "Wish I'd sucked that thing before I painted it."

I was lucky. On the wedding night which followed, I discovered that Joy had not gotten off so easily. Somebody had shaved her, too, down there in the good spot.

But even worse she had been permanently tattooed.

On the inside of her right thigh was a sign with a little arrow pointing you know where. The sign read:

24-HOUR PARKING.

86

And on the inside of her left thigh was another sign with an arrow pointing down her leg. This sign said: THANK YOU. CALL AGAIN.
Both signs were easy to read when you were headed for your dinner.

Going on the tour gave me a chance to get a whole new set of friends. Except for Spec Reynolds at Goat Hills and one or two other people I thought I'd had about all of Fort Worth I could stand until I came back in the next life as a grasshopper or an independent oil man.

It's probably a judgment call on the part of the official whether Donny Smithern was a step up or a step down for me. I have to admit, however, that getting to know Donny when I first came out here was a big help.

Donny is a stylish person on the surface, and I learned a good deal about the tour very quickly just being able to loaf with him. In other words, I learned things about how to pack, what tournaments to skip, the best places to stay, where the good restaurants were, who to know, who not to know, and maybe even a little bit about who to unknow.

When a guy is a rookie everyone he meets around a country club who wears a tournament-committee blazer and has a suntan seems to be somebody important. Most of them aren't. They only want to bore you with stories about their own golf games, and then introduce you to another idiot as if you're their new best friend.

In my first month on the tour I was with Donny one day at Indian Wells in Palm Springs when this committeeman in his blazer and dumb hat started to tell us about a charity pro-am he'd played in with Dave Eichelberger. "On the first hole . . ." he said.

Donny grinned nicely enough and said, "Hey, wait a second, pal. If I have to go the whole eighteen, I've got to get caddy fees."

You don't really want to insult any of these people on the tournament committees, or make enemies of them. A lot of them have worked hard to organize the event, sell it to the public, and maybe even raise the prize money we play for. They're all members of the clubs where the tournaments are played, and most of them seem genuinely happy to see you every year.

But as I've heard Donny say, "That doesn't give the son of a bitch a right to drill a hole through me."

You learn to be nimble, is all I'm trying to say.

One afternoon at Westchester Country Club, during the Westchester Classic, merely a $600,000 heist for us, this stuttering committeeman with an Ivy League lisp said to Donny, "I-I . . . w-watched you today w-with El Nicko . . . P-pretty t-terrific, I-I thought."

Donny said thanks.

Then the guy said, "W-what a-are your plans for d-dinner?"

Donny glanced at me quickly and said:

"Was that a page for me just then? Did you hear that?"

"Think so," I said.

The committeeman said, "W-what w-was w-what?"

"I'd better get that phone call," Donny said.

And we did our vanishing act, leaving the committeeman alone with his insights into El Nicko's golf game.

I have a whole list of people now, from coast to coast, that I don't ever want to be trapped at dinner with. If they don't mutilate you with tales of their new graphite shafts, then they'll solid put you into a full snore with anecdotes from the dazzling world of the savings-and-loan business.

Some of their wives are worse. If they don't happen to drink too much and force you to dance to an orchestra that sounds like a piano-tuning contest, they don't drink at all and make your eyes blur with their plans for re-modeling the clubhouse dining room.

Donny Smithern never minded the wives if they were halfway good-looking because Donny is a dedicated swordsman, and age rarely made any difference to him.

I once asked Donny how he could get enthusiastic about making it with one of those clacking, country-club dolls who only talked about curtains and drapes.

"Duty," he said.

Donny always enjoyed long-range projects. When he found one he kind of liked, he would work on becoming good friends with her husband. Then he would start to produce extra clubhouse badges for them. Or he might even go so far as to volunteer free golf lessons for their rotten teenage sons.

Ultimately he would become a close friend of the family, being the only "celebrity" they knew.

It might take him a year, two years, to consolidate the relationship, but finally the opportunity would present itself—and Donny would score another golden oldie.

He has argued with me that it was worth all of the

trouble. "Besides, it's noble to spread cheer," he says.

Often, it is not so much trouble. There are wives around Palm Springs and Fort Lauderdale, and places like that, who are slicker than a damp grip. And if you aren't careful you might find yourself getting laid at Sunday brunch. Some of it's there for any of us. Not just Donny.

Also, there are places where the logistics are perfect for getting it on. Places where we might be staying right at the club where the tournament's being played. At Pebble Beach Lodge, for example, or Doral, or a La Costa.

It is no brilliant stunt for Donny to cruise off to his room with an overripe lady whose husband is excited about being out on the course following Nicklaus.

Donny has a simple explanation for why there are all these indoor athletes around. Which is:

"Hell, once they get rich and their kids are half-grown, what else are they gonna do besides play Slip Off and Trick Fuck?"

Donny was the first player on the tour to wear his hair long, over his ears, and also to grow a mustache. Then he was the first golf pro to get a spiked hair cut and shave off his mustache. There's no question that he's made himself a personality slightly larger than his golfing ability.

He still has his clothes specially made so he can dress differently from the rest of us. His slacks, shirts, sweaters, and shoes come out in such colors as burnt orange, faded lime, asphalt gray, surf-foam white, Dunhill gold, and corned-beef pink.

He was the first pro to wear a pair of patent leather Gucci golf shoes. He also introduced epaulets to the rain suit.

"When I walk down the fairway I want the lovelies to know it's me for sure," Donny once explained. "How do you think I'd look in tinted goggles?"

He has such confidence as a swordsman he's set goals for himself which most guys would consider impossible.

One of his early goals was to get laid on a commercial flight. I know he accomplished it because I was with him. I saw a stewardess follow him into the john shortly after the movie came on. I put the clock on them. Twenty minutes. And Donny came out giving me the thumbs up.

He later decided that the only real challenge for a player of his stature would be to get laid in first class, *not* during a movie, *not* in the john, and *not* on a 747 where you could move around, upstairs and all. And to make it more severe, he said, you would have to do it while your wife was traveling with you.

I said he would need some luck on that one.

Donny claims he handled the case coming back from the Hawaiian Open on the red-eye from Honolulu to Los Angeles. He got a good break when the flight wasn't crowded, he said, and he got another one when a woman on board turned out to be a golf fan who was impressed with him.

All he had to do then was pour enough wine down Katie to make her go to sleep, wait for the crew to turn out the lights, and move back a couple of rows.

He got the woman drinking pretty good. Or as Donny

put it, "A Drambuie front moved in." Then he took out the armrest, reached up and grabbed a blanket, and that was it.

"I'll never forget old 6-A and -B," he likes to say, with a trace of nostalgia.

Donny once confessed to me why he thought he had so much success with women. I don't remember having asked about it.

It was almost in the form of a lecture, as if I was going through a learning program.

"Let's don't kid around about it," he said. "I'm a handsome guy. Maybe a little decadent looking. But that's okay. I use it. You've got to look 'em in the eye. Ever notice how I always look 'em in the eye when I'm talking, or lighting their cigarette? That's important."

"Right," I said. "If I were a woman and you were talking to me but looking across the room at Andy Williams, I'd be pissed."

"Being able to appear sincere is another big thing," Donny said. "Also, I have the ability to flatter. Sincerity and flattery. Never underestimate their importance."

Never, I said.

"Here's another thing," he said. "Patience. I worked four years on one in San Francisco. It was worth it. Believe me. Persistence goes along with patience, in a way. I've got both. If you're persistent, you're interested. If you're interested, you're sincere. See what I mean?"

Was that all?

"Only one other thing," Donny said. "Dependable,

vitamin-strengthened hard-ons. You can't disappoint 'em. Word gets around."

"Aw, I see," I said. "You're talking about *fuckin'*. Hell, I didn't know people did that anymore."

The truth about Donny Smithern is that he's never cared about anybody but himself. Maybe if you were a blind man and Donny wasn't in a real big hurry he would pull you out of a ditch. But like most everybody I've ever known who grew up rich in southern California, Donny has this philosophy that says you've got to fuck the world before it fucks you because the rest of the world wants to fuck everybody who has fancy clothes, no acne, and palm trees in the yard.

I don't know why so many people from California have this notion, unless, as Beverly Tidwell once said, the Hollywood Republicans insisted that it was taught in the schools. You would think that with California being the land of plenty, in terms of everyone being blond and tan and healthy on the tits, it would encourage Californians to be generous.

Donny, for instance, grew up at Bel Air Country Club. His family was well-off. He was good-looking. He had talent. He had delicious sisters. He didn't know anybody but movie stars, aerospace executives, and maître d's.

"That's the trouble," Beverly said. "People like Donny can't wait to reach voting age so they can try to get the death penalty instituted for anybody who doesn't know how to Simonize a Bentley properly."

I had this discussion one day with Donny about paying

caddies, I recall. It was after I'd seen him give his caddy an absurdly small amount of money for a week's work.

"Piss on 'em," he said. "If they haven't got any more ambition than to be caddies, they don't deserve any better."

I wondered what he would pay a good caddy. One that might have helped him a lot.

"If a caddy can help you, then you don't know how to play golf," he said.

I asked Donny what he thought a good caddy on the tour was supposed to do?

He said, "Keep his mouth shut, keep your clubs clean, not steal your balls, and try not to be a nigger."

"I have to admire your compassion," I said.

Donny said, "Let me tell you something, Kenny. If you start worrying about compassion, you're not going to be a competitor. If you're going to win out here, you've got to hate the golf course, and everybody who's trying to beat you."

I suggested that the tour was such a good deal, there was enough prize money for all of us.

He said, "There's not enough for *me*. The government's always going to take half of what you make and give it to the niggers."

I pointed out that he seemed to be living rather well. Had a big house in Dallas, a cute wife, and he was fairly famous. He was a real problem for society.

"What's Katie got to do with anything?" he said. "I could win me another one of those at Houston, or the week after."

Excuse me, I said. Thought he loved his wife.

"Christ," Donny said. "Love is a two-hundred-eighty-yard drive and a seven-iron four feet from the pin."

I only stared at him, wondering if he believed that.

Then he said, "But you might miss the fucking putt. That's why you've got to hate everything."

In other words, I said, his theory was that you had to be a bad-ass or you weren't a real competitor?

He said, "What I do on the golf course depends on me, and nobody else. So the less shit I have to take from anybody—about *anything*—it's bound to help my game."

As far as mankind was concerned, I said, I wondered if Donny's outlook was the best?

"Fuck mankind," he said. "Just let me make some birdies."

•   •   •

Four

WHEN A NEW GUNNER comes out on the tour with a big amateur reputation, there are a bunch of players like Donny who can't wait to try to fuck him up. He's a threat, obviously, to their incomes.

They did a fine job on Grover Scomer.

When Grover came out here, he had a smooth swing and plenty of confidence, and he had won everything there was to win as a world-class amateur.

Grover is a tall, stout, good-natured fellow who's finally made it, to a degree, but he still hasn't become the big winner that was predicted of him because he's awed by the tour and he *thinks* too much.

He came out with this tremendous natural ability, having won the British Amateur and the Western and the Trans-Miss, and all that kind of thing I never got to play in, and right away he started listening to anybody who cared to discuss hitting through the "power zone."

I said to him once, "Grover, don't listen to anybody out here, including me."

But he would ask me the damndest questions.

For instance, Grover asked me one time whether I inhaled or exhaled on my backswing.

One of the first things somebody told him on the tour was not to wear a glove. With his large hands he didn't need a glove, they said. Did Hogan or Nelson ever wear a glove? Of course not.

Well, that took about twenty yards off his tee ball right there.

They changed his grip. They told him he should start walking faster between shots on the par fives, and he ought to walk slower on the par threes. Told him he ate too much breakfast and not enough lunch. Told him he should wear dark shirts in hot weather "to hold in the heat." Told him his backswing had a tendency to go past "horizontal." Told him he needed to get himself a light-weight putter for fast greens, which is just the opposite of what you want.

Grover used to think about all of this so much he got to where he would hardly speak when you had dinner with him. He would just sit there and look off.

Occasionally he would blink and say something weird like, "What's more important? To be able to hit it or aim it?"

At Jacksonville once, during the Tournament Players Championship, I found him hitting practice shots in the dark. He frowned at me and said:

"Donny claims you can actually feel it when your wedges are going to nestle."

I said, "Grover, these guys are only trying to jack you around. Don't ever listen to Donny unless he's telling you how to fuck the girl behind the Hertz counter."

One week Grover would think he'd finally discovered the secret because he would finish twelfth or something, but the following week he'd miss the cut. He'd shoot an unreal round for you now and then. He once laid a young 63 on Harbour Town, and led. But he shot an 88 the next day, and went on to Greensboro.

He said to me one day, "When you're standing over a short putt, Kenny, do you pretend the cup's a bucket?"

Of course not, I said.

He said, "Do you pretend it's a thimble?"

I said shit no.

He said, "Do you ever find yourself standing over a putt and looking at your shoes, wishing you'd worn another pair?"

I could only squint at him.

Grover said, "Have you ever stood over a putt and wondered how many microscopic bugs were looking up at you?"

I glanced down at the ground.

And he said, "I had an eight-inch putt today, Kenny, and as I was getting ready to tap it in, I thought to myself that right there where I was standing—right there underneath my brown and white Footjoys—I was probably crushing to death a whole civilization of living things. You know what happened?"

I sure didn't.

99

Grover said, "This impulse came over me as I took the putter back, and instead of tapping the ball in, I took the club back some more, and I hit myself in the right foot with it. Hard as I could. My caddy said he thought he heard me mumbling, 'Murderer, murderer,' to myself. Under my breath."

I asked him what happened to the eight-inch putt.

"I don't know," Grover said. "I withdrew."

Grover is a very popular guy among the players today because he's still as much of a fan as he is a competitor. But he's probably become a closer friend of mine than anyone else's. A long time ago we discovered that we were the two biggest country-music freaks on the tour. I've learned a lot of golf history from him. And he's learned a lot about how to play the game from me.

When he was fresh out of the University of Colorado and all those amateur victories, it used to piss off Donny that I would bring Grover with me so often at night.

"What do you want that dumb-ass around for?" Donny would say. "He can't get out of his own way."

I would answer that Grover looked up to Donny as a player, and Donny ought to be nicer to him.

"He makes me nervous," Donny would say. "He's always butting in when I'm working on a chick. He's asking her who she knows in Boulder."

Donny finally had it sink in that Grover was going to be around pretty often in the evenings with us if I noticed that Grover seemed lonesome and had nothing to do.

So Donny decided he could make some use of the situation because Grover was single. Use him as a beard, is what Donny thought he'd do.

Any number of times when Katie was traveling with Donny, an old friend of Donny's would wind up being escorted by Grover when the six of us would go to dinner. Donny, Katie, Janie Ruth, me, Grover—and the lovely and charming Pam, Pattie, Betsy, Susie, Hilary, Andrea, Myra, Cheryl, or whoever.

Two years ago when we were in Fort Lauderdale for the Inverrary Classic Donny worked for two days to get one of his all-stars to drive up from Miami Beach to have dinner with us. She would be with Grover, of course, but Donny promised her we would go somewhere so the two of them could at least dance together and perhaps sit next to each other so they could thigh-swap, under the table. And who was to say that they might not be able to go to the powder rooms simultaneously, and thereby slip off for a ten-minute moonshot?

Donny selected a wonderful place called Captain Hook's on the intercoastal waterway. It had a dance floor the size of a throw rug with seven thousand people trying to get on it. It had a three-piece combo with seventeen amplifiers which could do a remarkable imitation of a nuclear holocaust. And it had the only hamburgers I've ever tried to eat with petty cash in them.

The girl from Miami Beach was a pile-driving, bone-crunching home-wrecker named Linda. Long black hair, sleepy blue eyes, body, attitude, moves. Wanted in eight states for murder.

Donny spoke to someone at Captain Hook's and got us

a table outdoors under an awning so we could be closer
to the humidity, and look across the waterway at several
condominiums locked in deadly battle.

The first thing Grover did was seat Linda at the opposite end of the table from Donny. And with the fallout of
the music reaching the outdoor terrace it was practically
impossible even to talk to the person sitting next to you
without cupping your hands and shouting.

Nevertheless, Donny tried to engage Linda in a conversation.

"Where are you from?" he hollered.

I could read his lips. Linda couldn't. She said:

"What?"

"Where . . . are . . . you . . . *from?*" Donny said
again.

"Great," said Linda. "Thank you."

Donny retreated to his cocktail. Katie sat there looking
around and smiling, as ever. Janie Ruth put her fingers
in her ears. And I watched Grover demonstrate the various ways to hold a golf club for Linda.

After a while Donny made another attempt. I thought
he sounded like a guy on the bridge of a schooner in the
fog.

"Are . . . you . . . from . . . around . . . here?"
Donny called out.

"I was," shouted Linda. "Now . . . I'm . . . divorced."

I said to Donny:

"Where . . . are . . . you . . . bound . . . for?"

He said, "*What?*"

I said, "Are . . . you . . . carrying . . . teak . . .
silks . . . ivory?"

The nuclear holocausts finally took an intermission. Everybody suggested a quieter place where we might go, but no one could think of anywhere that wouldn't require a forty-five-minute drive.

Grover said, "What's wrong with where we are?"

Donny said, "If I could move away from this chair. That music is coming right at me. Maybe if I was at the other end of the table . . ."

"Why don't you come on down here when they start up again?" Grover said. "Linda and I are gonna dance, anyway."

Donny got out a cigarette.

I made hand signals toward a waitress telling her to do everything for the table again—twice.

Then Donny said, "Uh, Linda . . . How long have you lived in Miami Beach?"

"Five years," Grover said. "She's originally from Akron. Hey, guess what? She's the hostess at the Candlelight Club on the causeway. We've been in there, haven't we? Kenny? Donny? Haven't we been in there?"

"I don't think I know the place," Donny said. "What's the name of it?"

"The Candlelight," said Linda, coolly. "It's near the Harbour Lounge. Very convivial. Informal, good food. It's mainly for married couples and families dining out."

"Sounds nice," Katie said.

"I know we've been in there before," Grover said. "Isn't that the place with all the shapely adorables?"

Donny excused himself to visit the men's room.

Linda excused herself to visit the ladies' room.

Donny was back in something like eight minutes.

103

Linda never returned. Grover conducted a search. He reported that he had found her in the parking lot getting into a taxi. Said she told him she had phoned her answering service in Miami Beach and there was an urgent message. Her uncle was arriving that night to spend a few days with her. He was probably there now.

"She said to tell everybody she was glad to have met us," Grover said.

The music started up again. Donny began to yawn and look at his watch.

I couldn't resist cupping my hands and saying to Donny:

"I . . . think . . . Linda's . . . uncle . . . plays . . . for . . . the . . . Dolphins."

At Heavenly Pines Grover Scomer had rotten luck. In the first round he had one tee shot hit a sprinkler head and ricochet into the water, and he had another shot come to rest with a pine cone sitting right behind it. All of this helped shove him up to a 79.

He needed to play pretty good in the second round to make the cut, and he did, most of the way. Looked like he might shoot a 70, or one or two over, with only a few holes to go, he said. But on the 16th he hit a shot into a bunker and it rolled down into a heelprint. Took him three to get it out. He shot a 73 and missed the cut by one.

In the locker room after I'd had my drinks with the New Yorkers, and after Donny had practiced, Grover came in and plopped down on a bench and sighed.

"I can hit out of river sand," he said, "but I'm never gonna learn how to get out of this silicone shit."

Donny and I were sitting at a big round table in the middle of the locker room. Some of the other players had been there and left, along with a couple of writers.

"Nobody's ever made a wedge where the flange will ride silicone very good," I said.

"You guys played good, huh?" Grover said.

"I hit sixteen greens," I said.

"Bullshit," Donny said. "You scrambled just like me. I was right behind you."

"I don't know what the hell's wrong with me," Grover said. "Damn, that's a tough golf course out there. I don't know how in the shit you guys are puttin' those numbers up."

"The greens are getting harder," I said. "It'll really be brutal these last two rounds."

"I got to get a new putter," said Grover. "I got to get off this center-shaft crap. There never was a great putter who didn't use a rear-shaft."

"How about Hogan?" I said.

"He was a greater *player* than he was a *putter*," Grover said.

"All those good ones could putt," Donny said. "There's never been a great player who couldn't putt."

"Except you," I grinned.

"That's *right*, goddamn it," Donny said. "How many long ones do you ever see me make? Hell, I never hole one of those road maps like you do. I don't three-putt that much, but I don't make any, either."

"You make your share," I said.

"Well, I don't," Grover said. "I got to get me a rear-shafted putter. I know that. Don't you have an old

Armour you aren't using, Donny? Let me try it out in Akron next week."

"I need it," Donny said.

"What for?" I said.

"I need it, that's all," Donny said. "If this George Low I've got turns to shit, I'll go to the Armour."

"I've got to find *something*," Grover said.

"No rule says you can't go in the pro shop and buy one," Donny said.

"Nobody can putt with a *new* putter," I said. "You've got to find you an old one that's been fooled around with and feels right. Let him try the Armour, Donny."

"I need it, I said," Donny repeated.

"What are you being such a prick for?" I said. "Here's a man who's done missed the cut, who's supposed to be a friend, and you don't want to help him out. Man, you're stronger than cat food."

"The Mex carries a bunch of 'em around with him," Grover said. "Maybe I can get one from him."

"It might not be the putter, Grover," I said. "You don't stay still, is what I think. You got to hold that head still and get a good rap on it."

Donny said, "Take that damn scalpel Nicklaus uses away from him, and we'd see how many major championships he'd win."

"Jack doesn't make that many putts," Grover said. "If you want to talk about somebody who's a much better player than he is a putter . . ."

"Where's his short game?" Donny said. "Let me see him hit the seven, eight, nine, and wedge. Let me see him in a bunker. Put him in trouble. Shit. The Mex can hit shots Jack's never even imagined. So can a lot of us."

"Yeah, that's right," I said. "I guess those twenty major championships he's won were just a rumor."

Donny said, "Jack's a great *thinker*, that's all. And he's got composure. But don't tell me the man can hit golf shots like some of the rest of us."

"He can hit a few for me, if he wants to," I said.

"Boy, you guys are right up there," Grover said. "Isn't that something? Hell, I'm not going to Akron till Monday. I've got to stay here and watch what happens to you guys."

"That's one of your troubles, Grover," Donny said. "Until you get over being a damn *aficionado* out here, you're never gonna win."

"If I went to Akron all I'd do is watch the Open on television," Grover said. "Might as well stay here and see it live."

Donny said, "If I'd missed the cut, my ass would already be on the road."

"Well, if it wasn't that you guys are friends of mine . . ." Grover said.

I said, "I'm flattered, Grover. Seriously. I just hope I can keep playing good enough to make it a contest for our ass-hole buddy here."

"If I start putting," Donny said, "you fuckers are history—because the hunt's over."

I looked at Grover and winked.

He smiled. Then he stood up and stretched.

"I got to pay off my caddy," he said. "Maybe I *will* look around in the pro shop. I got to get a damn putter somewhere."

Golf may have driven more people crazy than women.

What was it that Bernard Darwin wrote once? I think it was something like, "It's the constant and undying hope for improvement that makes golf so exquisitely worth the playing."

I read that out of a book to Janie Ruth one evening and she said, "Them fuckin' English know how to diddle the words, don't they?"

Watching poor old Grover Scomer out here always reminded me of a guy who hung around Goat Hills with us. Willard Peacock. He never had a chance to beat anybody, and he never should have been in all those gambling games, but he loved pain, I guess.

Willard Peacock drove a delivery truck for Grandma's Crunchies, which was a company that made cookies and sold them to cafes and drugstores. Willard couldn't have earned much money but what he made he usually lost to us at Goat Hills.

If you were getting low on cash and you happened to be driving around Goat Hills and you saw the Grandma's Crunchies truck hidden behind the tall hedge near the clubhouse, you stomped on the brakes, hopped out of your car, grabbed your sticks, donned your cleats, and went looking for Willard.

You could give Willard any advantage—one up, two up, three up, four up—and beat him so bad he'd have to be put in a crate and sent to the State Fair. Sooner or

later in the course of a game he'd have a temper fit and
start trying to see how much he could lose if he really
tried.

I saw Spec Reynolds offer him *five up* once on nine
holes for $50. Which meant that Willard had to win
because he'd be five holes ahead with only four to play
before they even teed off. But Willard couldn't decide
whether to take the bet.

Spec Reynolds was a crafty soul, and Willard figured
there just had to be a trick to it some way.

Spec had a reputation for being able to outbet folks,
regardless of what he might shoot. And he was a master
at inventing crazy games he could win at. He could play
golf better than any of us on one leg, or with one club.
He could putt better with a nine-iron than he could with
a putter.

He could chip with a three-wood, hit sand shots with
a two-iron, hit a ball blindfolded or with an R.C. Cola
bottle. And he could see in the dark.

He showed up once with a cast on his leg. Claimed his
leg was broken. Kept the cast on for six weeks and played
golf by paying a black kid to haul him around the course
in a little red wagon. Spec got a lot of sympathy bets,
with considerable advantages built in, from everybody
but me. I knew the leg wasn't broken.

Spec would bet on anything. Rain. Sunshine. How
many people would be wearing blue suits on Sunday at
the Travis Avenue Baptist Church. I was with him once
when we walked in to count them. And I still can't
imagine why Rev. J. Frank Buford thought we'd come in
to get baptized in our knit shirts, visors, khakis, and golf
gloves.

He would bet on how old the meat loaf was in some kind of diner near Ardmore, Oklahoma, or how many towels had gone on sale at Dillard's department store, or how many people would get killed in Chevrolets on Texas highways over a holiday weekend. He would have researched all of these things, of course.

Spec was dangerous, and that's why Willard worried about taking five up on nine holes. There had to be something else to it, Willard said.

"Yeah, if I win the front, then I got to play you for $100, double up, on the back," Willard said.

Spec said, "No you don't. I'm just tryin' to give you back some of your money."

Willard said, "You're talking about five strokes, then. Not five holes."

"Nope," said Spec.

Willard said, "You mean you want to give me five holes *up* on only nine to play? At Goat Hills? Today?"

"That's right," Spec said.

Willard said, "Why don't you just *give* me $50?"

Spec said, "Well, I thought we'd go out and enjoy this pretty day."

Willard said, "Yeah, you're gonna get me out there and then bet me on how many sparrows are sittin' on a telephone wire or somethin'."

"No I'm not," Spec grinned.

"Let me get this straight," Willard said. "I've got five up on nine holes . . . in the game of golf . . . with you . . . *against* you, I mean . . . at Goat Hills . . . today . . . for $50. And I don't have to play you on the back nine? And I don't have to play you ever again at golf . . . or no other game?"

"That's it," said Spec.
Willard Peacock looked at Spec for a long time. And
Willard said:
"I don't like it. No bet."

The thing that made Willard go insane on the golf
course would be to slice the ball. Which was just about
the only kind of shot he ever hit. A rainbow ball.
At first, his temper would boil slowly.
He would swing and hit another slice, out of bounds
perhaps, over the homes of Rotarians across the street.
A few holes later you might see him put a ball in his
mouth and bite down on it, making a humming noise.
Then he would turn his torture directly toward the
clubs. With the irons, he would hit rocks. And with the
woods, he would mash his cleats into the tops of them as
he stood around awaiting his turn to tee off.
"How does *that feel?*" Willard would ask his driver,
pressing on it with his foot. "Feel good? Want some
more?"
Eventually he would hit one of those slices that would
really put him in jail. Down in a creek bed with all the
mud and water moccasins.
All bets would suddenly look hopeless. Originals,
presses, everything.
Willard would deliberately and slowly raise his driver
up to his face and say something to it in a soft voice
which we always thought sounded like a good imitation
of James Cagney. He would say:
"Fuck you . . . and ever thing . . . you stand for."
This would be the signal for the rest of us to take
cover.

We would dive behind golf carts, squat behind our bags, lay flat on the ground, or sprint for the nearest tee shed.

Taking the rest of his clubs out of his bag and throwing them in all directions, Willard would start cussing, and the thing about his cussing was, he would be so outraged and spewing out the words so fast, they wouldn't make sense.

"Sumbitchin' cock-mother shit-bat game," he would yell. "Crap-suck, jibby-gap, slice'n bastard, bubber-dop, shack-suck nigger-spick!"

For a moment Willard would get calm. He would tee up a ball, take a proper stance, waggle the club, and look serious.

It was like being in the eye of the hurricane.

"Last chance," he would say to the ball and club. "You just think about this real good. I mean, this is *it*. I'm gonna take one more swing and if you slice on me . . ."

Willard would take his usual cut at the ball, and it would slice so wildly it would look as if it might come back and hit him if it could stay in the air long enough.

"Aw, goddamn," he'd say. "Aw, goddamn shit. Aw, goddamn shit piss crap."

By now he would have Tabasco in his eyes.

"Aw, goddamn shit piss crap . . . fuckin' turd-dim, rotten, son of a bapper-ding, gipe-back fucker shit!" he would cry.

He would pound the club on the ground, as if he were trying to kill a scorpion.

"Miserable daddy-dank bastard fuckin' dippy-prick shit singin' cock-mother MacGregor fump slimy piss-heel fucker munk stoppy blap suck spick nigger," he'd shout.

By this time, of course, Spec Reynolds and T. Lou (Tiny) Fawver and Hope-I-Do Collins and me and whoever else was around would be laughing so hard we would honestly need an ambulance.

Sometimes Willard would take a four-iron or some kind of club out to the street and start scraping it on the concrete curb. Ruthlessly.

And he would growl, "Blister your fuckin' ass *raw*, is what I'll do, you shit-stinkin' piece of stainless steel pile of shit-stinkin' cocker bap!"

Finally, Willard would be exhausted. He would leisurely gather up all of his clubs, even the ones in two pieces, and stuff them back in his bag. Then he would stand there, panting. He would light a cigarette. And he would start to look around for the rest of us.

And he would say:

"Well, goddamn it. Are we gonna play golf, or are we just gonna stand around?"

Beverly used to love the stories about my Goat Hills days. It was the thing she liked best about golf, I think. If not the only thing.

I entertained her with them as a way of telling her about myself.

I was honest with her from the moment we met. Told her that what she saw and what she heard was all there was to me.

There wasn't any hidden genius anywhere, I said. All I knew anything about was golf and one or two card games. Went all the way through Paschal High without even a textbook or a locker, which you could do if you lettered in a major sport like football or basketball.

Said I went through two years at TCU on a golf scholarship, and the only good grade I ever made in anything
was a B-minus in American history because the profes-
sor, Mr. Robinson, thought he could play golf a little—
and I conducted a funeral for him one day at Goat Hills.

Never remembered going to class very often in anything else. And the only reason I ever dropped by Mr.
Robinson's class was to find out if he had any cash on
him that he owed me, or whether he could squeeze in
nine holes that day before dark.

I met Beverly in Dallas one day when I accidentally
wandered into a place called The Third World Rip-Off.
I was looking for some change for the parking meter but
I got Bev instead, along with a cup of Turkish coffee.

The Third World Rip-Off was supposed to be an art
gallery, I think, but all I saw was some Apache jewelry,
sketches of what I presumed to be urban-renewal projects, and assorted driftwood. There were also some
dresses hanging on a pipe that were made out of quilts
and cheesecloth.

There was some loud music playing which sounded
like folk-rock-country-soul poetry. As near as I could figure, the lyrics dealt with junk food, freeways and legaliz-
ing cocaine. A large sign on the wall said:

DALLAS EATS REINFORCED CONCRETE.

Beverly was good-looking in a no-makeup kind of way.
She had a trim body, appropriately curved. She had
long, straight, brown hair, parted in the middle, with
glasses on top of it. She had graceful moves. The kind
where you knew things came easy for her. She had on a

loose cotton sweater and a pair of snug jeans that looked like they'd been to several rodeos.

"You the owner?" I said. "I'm trying to find an American flag."

She offered me some coffee and we sat down to chat. Obviously I didn't get up again for about four years.

It didn't take very long for us to get in the sack together. I was her first athlete and she was my first rich society dropout. I will have to give Bev credit for introducing me to my first marijuana cigarette, my first Dexamyl, my first vibrator, and my first amyl nitrite. All I ever introduced her to was a challenge.

In our early days Bev was real sweet. She would stare at me on occasion and say something like, "Have I said thank you lately, Ken?"

She would be thanking me for "saving" her from what she always thought was her destiny. Marrying your normal Dallas nitwit who only cared about real estate developments, the country club dance, and buying clothes.

"No one cares about how things are," she would say. "They only care about the way things seem."

I told her once I couldn't put that philosophy together with those amyl nitrites she stuffed up my nose when we were making love.

"Planned ecstasy is an altogether different subject," she would say.

Bev's father, the ever-popular, crowd-pleasing Mr. Chub Tidwell, SMU '51, was delighted his daughter wanted to marry a golf pro. He said it was the first "pro-America" idea she'd ever had.

For a wedding present he gave us an apartment in a

new complex he had built, plus four hundred shares in a data-computer stock that went farther south than Buenos Aires.

My last honest effort to talk Bev out of marrying me was a lecture on all of her artistic interests.

All I knew about sculpture, I said, was that most of it was done by fag Greeks who seemed to prefer big asses and small tits on women.

Painting, I said, was okay as long as the painter didn't try to make you guess whether it was a picture of the Hill Country or kitchen linoleum.

I told her the only music I appreciated was cowboy, and I didn't recall that old Billy Joe Mozart or Connie Fay Beethoven had written much of it.

Poetry, I said, was just a case of old Robert Browning asking old Elizabeth Barrett if she wanted to fuck—but making it rhyme.

Said I'd never been to any ballet, of course, but there couldn't be any of those little interior decorators, or mean-ass Lesbians, who could dance any better than your average, street-corner Philadelphia spade.

My favorite American authors, I said, were a few guys who could write about sports and gangsters and make it funny. And in terms of the literary classics, I said, I'd probably go with the books that were the longest and the dullest because they would be thick and help fill up the shelves.

And that was all I knew, I said, about your lively arts.

Bev only gave me a kiss and said:

"In . . . fucking . . . credible."

The best way to indoctrinate Bev to the golf tour, I

thought, would be to start her off in the most enchanting, glamorous place I knew of. The Monterey Peninsula. By taking her to the Bing Crosby National Pro-Am I figured there would be a lot of diversions for her. She wouldn't necessarily have to watch the golf.

She could prowl through all of the shops in Carmel, or drive up to Big Sur, or even hang around the Pebble Beach Lodge and giggle at all of the movie stars.

I made a point of booking us into the Pine Inn, right there in Carmel, in the middle of all of those Dutch door joints—the art galleries with portraits of saucer-eyed children and seals gobbling abalone, and all of the rustic, ye olde eateries where you're supposed to be stunned by the delicacy of somebody's spinach souffle or tomato aspic.

I thought Bev would like the Pine Inn because it has a musty, intellectual feeling to it, with a lot of old men and women creeping around in tweed coats.

I had told her the Crosby tournament wasn't so important in the big picture of the tour. It was closer to a social event because the pros generally drew amateur partners who carried flasks and had golf swings that would screw them ankle-deep in the mud.

Unless you're Nicklaus or Trevino, you have to tee off at 7 A.M. out there. This means rain and cold and a wind that will sometimes blow you all the way to an artichoke field in Salinas. And it can take up to six hours to play eighteen holes because you're frequently playing behind a singer or comedian who can't seem to get his feet untangled from the ice plant.

Unfortunately, our first trip to the Crosby was before I rated a celebrity partner like Jack Lemmon. This was

PART 2

back in the days when I would draw me a guy from Tampa, who would have gotten into the tournament because Robert Stack caught the flu.

The guy from Tampa would be just as disappointed to get *me* for a partner, having dreamed of a John Mahaffey or a Donny Smithern.

There was an indication that I had made a mistake taking Bev to the Crosby the first time we drove from Carmel to Pebble Beach. We were riding along on part of the 17 Mile Drive, and she kept looking at some of those big homes in the forest which have cute names on signs. Things like "Shank-rila," and "Fair-a-way Haven," and "Pino O'Fore," and "The Back Tease."

I tried to explain what those names meant.

"My God," Bev said quietly. "Some people make golf their whole lives."

My first round in the tournament with Bev following me was a noteworthy experience.

On the first green at Pebble Beach I missed a birdie putt from about six feet. So she came over to the tee on the second hole and said:

"What in the world did you do that for?"

I said I sure hadn't tried to do it.

"You were *this* close," she said. "That's dumb."

It was a terrible mistake, I said. No question about it.

She said, "Well, that's enough of *that*, okay?"

I looked bored. Which she noticed.

"Look, if you don't want me out here, just say so," she said.

118

I said she might want to just stroll around and get the feel of things. Learn by observing. Maybe not talk to me so much. I would be trying to concentrate.

"On what?" she said.

The thing which came to my mind was the old golf joke about the man trying to explain the game to his wife. He took her out to a long par-three hole, put a ball down, and hit it. Sure enough, the ball went into the cup for the first hole-in-one of his life. But the wife didn't even react. She thought that was the object of it all.

A couple of holes later I found myself in a sand trap, digging my heels in, when Beverly leaned across the ropes and hollered at me.

"That's sand," she said. "Surely you don't have to hit the ball out of *that*."

I stared at her.

"Why don't you pick it up and drop it over your shoulder like that other man did a while ago?" she said.

I climbed out of the bunker and started toward her as she was saying, "Throw it out on the grass, Silly."

Briefly I explained a few things about the rules.

"I'm only trying to understand, Ken," she said. "You told me I could help you. That *is* what you said, isn't it?"

She went along keeping a safe distance for almost the rest of the round. Every now and then if she thought I was looking at her she would wave.

What finally did it was when our foursome got around to the 16th hole. My Tampa man and I were paired with

Ed Sneed and a young guy from Palm Beach that everybody called "El Richo."

I was not playing exceptionally well. Think I was about four over at the time. I know I had a good chance for a birdie on the 16th, and I was crouched down behind the ball, lining it up, when I heard Beverly yelling.

"Ken, quick!" she said.

I raised up, and looked around.

"Over there!" she shouted. "At the edge of the trees. Look at the deer!"

Well, if you know anything about the golf courses on the Peninsula—Pebble Beach or Cypress Point or Spyglass Hill—you know that occasionally a deer will run across the fairway.

I just hit the putt without even trying to make it. Then I missed the next one. And then I raked the ball in for another bogey.

And I went over to Bev, no hotter than the inside of your shirt on an August day in Texas.

"Fuck the deer," I said. "Fuck every goddamn deer on the whole fuckin' Monterey Peninsula."

Bev looked startled.

I said, "Fuck the deer and fuck the birds and fuck the seals and fuck the fuckin' abalone, and fuck every rich motherfucker who ever lived on 17 fuckin' Mile Drive."

Bev kept looking at me.

"Fuck all those Dutch doors, too," I said. "Fuck Big Sur. Fuck this whole Route I, gingerbread, fairy tale, antique, overquaint, Shangri-la pile of fuckin' shit."

She couldn't help smiling.

And she said, "It's Willard Peacock, folks."

I just looked off, steaming.

Then I said, "Bev, I'm not mad at you. I'm really not. How are you supposed to know there's a fuckin' deer around here? I'm mad at my fuckin' self for being distracted and frustrated."

I said, "You've got to understand that this is the hardest fuckin' game in the world to play real good. You've got to play your ass off just to get by."

After a pause she said:

"I could accept that if you hadn't told me Arnold Palmer has his own private jet."

Something about the atmosphere of the "resort community" of Heavenly Pines had kept me thinking about Beverly all during the National Open. I think it was the forced quaintness of the place, similar to Carmel's, only newer.

And she had naturally been very much on my mind because of her illness.

That Friday night your genial, 36-hole-Open leader decided he'd better not go out on the town. There were several restaurants within walking distance of the Heavenly Marriott South. They all had names like The Fox & Goose, or The Hounds & Trumpets, or something like that.

And Dutch doors.

"Just so we don't eat in the room," Janie Ruth said. "I hate all them plastic dishes. Besides, it's fun to go out in public with you leadin' this thing."

I waited until Janie Ruth went to the shopping area off of the hotel lobby to spend her daily hour in Carolina Cathy's boutique. And I did what I had been wanting to do for several days. Phone Bev.

121

I reached her in her room at the Turtle Creek Medical Center in Dallas.

"Hidy," I said. "This here's your favorite ex-husband."

In a slow, deep, theatrically country voice she said:

"Hi, there, roughrider. Here's a little song I wrote when me and the whole family had Big C. I'd like to sing it for you right now. It's called 'You Sprayed My Heart with a Can of Raid So Why Can't You Swat My Lung?' "

I asked Bev if everything was true that I'd heard from Katie? That the doctors had put her in that particular hospital because it happened to have one of the few *Linac* machines in the world? A linear accelerator or something like that? Some kind of a radiation deal which might be able to shrink that motherfucker in her lung?

"Katie says the tumor's got the Big M," I said. "I just can't goddamn believe it."

"It's got something," Bev said. "It's about the size of a grapefruit."

I asked her what all this meant, actually?

She said, "Well . . . It's too big to operate on. That's the bad thing right now. But the radiologist says there's some real hope—no kidding—that the treatments will shrink it down to a manageable size. It's happened, they say. In other words, if it shrinks they can take it out. Of course . . . there might be a primary source."

I asked how she felt?

She said, "The treatments hurt like hell. But, Ken . . . honestly . . . I don't feel like a person who's only got . . . shit . . . a couple of months left, in case the son of a bitch won't shrink."

122

Two months? I said. Was she joking?

She said, "I just don't accept it, Ken. I really don't. Hey. Guess what? I've named it Donny."

Named what Donny? I said.

"This thing in the X-ray at the foot of my bed," she said. "Don't you think Donny's a good name for something as lousy as cancer?"

I said, "Bev, I just can't tell you how much that fuckin' word makes my back hurt and my chest hurt and my arm hurt."

She said, "It's not shrinking yet, Ken, but at least it isn't getting any larger. And it hasn't spread."

That might be a good sign, I said.

"Yeah," she said, "because you know why it hasn't? I'm thinking it away. That's why."

It could be done, I said.

"Damn right," said Bev. "The mind can accomplish anything. I mean, most people, when they find out they've got the queen of diamonds, they start singing hymns, trying to woo the Old Skipper."

"You sound pretty cheerful," I said.

She went on, "I am personally going to *command* Donny to shrivel up to the size of a Titleist, or something, and then I'm going to have it removed—and take up tennis again."

I said you couldn't beat her attitude.

"I'm serious," she said. "I told Katie that I'm only thirty-one and I'm pretty terrific, all around, and the Big C can get ready to put up the dukes."

I chuckled.

"You know what else?" she said. "After I whip the

123

bastard, head to head, and score one of the major upsets in the history of medical follies, I'm going to write a raging best seller."

I would read it, I said, if it was a thin book with a lot of pictures in it.

She said, "It's going to be the heart-warming story of how a brave, wonderful, witty, attractive, full-of-life young girl took on the Big M singlehandedly . . ."

"And exposed the disease as a plot against humanity involving the Republican Party and the A.M.A.," I said.

She laughed.

"Something like that," she said.

I said, "Listen, Bev. Is there anything I can do? Seriously?"

She said, "I haven't finished. After I write the best seller I'm going to get a tit job and buy some clinging outfits, and go on all the talk shows and become a literary slut."

Excellent, I said. Was her hair still long?

"Yes," she said. "I may have it streaked for TV. And put on some big round tinted glasses, like all of the other writers. Anyhow, I figure I will either be offered my own TV show or at the very least a syndicated column. But either way, I'll become fulfilled and more famous—and surely more influential—than Arnold Palmer. Which, in the end, would get me even with your dumb sport."

I was laughing when she added:

"I've got a good title. I'm going to call it *Nice Try, Big C, But You Had No Lick in the Stretch*. By the in . . . fucking . . . comparable Beverly Tidwell."

I asked again if there was anything I could do.

She said, "Come visit me after you win the Open. It would be neat to see you. I'm sure Janie Ruth wouldn't mind—unless she thinks it's contagious."

I said I would definitely come to Dallas. But winning the Open wasn't going to be so easy. I had two more rounds to play and a lot of gunners were right on my ass. Including Donny.

Bev said, "Do me a favor and finish ahead of Mr. Wonderful, at least. Will you?"

I said Donny was still one of her loves, right?

"How *is* the synthetic prick, anyway?" she asked.

"Oh," I said, "he's just your basic faded lime on Dunhill gold."

She said, "Tell him he's been immortalized in a Dallas X-ray."

I said I would. I also said I thought I heard Janie Ruth at the door. I'd call her again tomorrow night. And I told her to hang in there.

Bev said, "Go get 'em, Ken. Fairways and greens."

I was going to tell Bev that she sounded like she knew something about golf for an instant, but Janie Ruth entered the room. So I said into the receiver:

"Uh . . . that's right, Operator. Rooms 414 and 416 at eight-thirty A.M. Thank you."

And of course I could hear Beverly whooping as I hung up.

Beverly never liked anything about Donny Smithern from the first moment she met him—and heard him make several references to "Arnold" and "Frank" and "Deano" and "Andy," as well as the Polo Lounge, Palm

125

Beach, his business manager, Ponte Vedra, his exhibition schedule, and stone crabs, all in a record-breaking six minutes.

"He's a beautiful friend," she used to say. "He'll always be there if he needs you."

Politically, of course, Bev and Donny had no chance to get along.

She told him once, "It's rather difficult to have a sensible discussion with anyone who learned his political science from Bob Hope."

Bev knew I didn't give a damn about politics. As far as I was concerned, nobody had a priority on fucking things up. I used to tell her the only difference I was aware of between Democrats and Republicans was that Republicans seemed to have lower handicaps and more sets of clubs while Democrats liked to bet more—and paid off quicker.

Bev delighted in going with me to places like Palm Springs and wearing campaign buttons which said things like:

FREE THE DESERT . . . SURF LA QUINTA.

I tried to act like it didn't bother me at first, but it's pretty difficult to play golf with a squirrel in your stomach.

Let me give you an example of what a fun-filled evening was like in those days.

About three years ago during the Houston Open our steady foursome—Donny, Katie, and us—got invited out to dinner to this slick restaurant in the Remington Hotel by two of the tournament committeemen and their wives. The minute I heard one of the Houston men was named Bubba, and discovered he was in the oil-well supply business—his company rented "drillin' collars and blow-out preventers"—I started wishing for an open window and a parachute.

Any grown man I'd ever come across who still went by the name of Bubba was usually accustomed to holding the floor throughout an evening and laying a lukewarm filibuster on you.

In the early part of the meal Bubba shared his views with us on a variety of topics. With what he considered to be uproarious humor he presented his arguments in support of air pollution and planned obsolescence and against equal opportunity and all forms of ecology.

"In other words," Bubba said, "I'm in favor of amnesty for the American businessman."

Bev took all this pretty well. She was quiet and calm. I was proud of her. But she began losing the twinkle in her eyes when Bubba took half an hour to tell us a story about checking into this expensive hotel in Atlanta. And how, all of a sudden, they stepped into this elevator crammed full of "niggers," and how they discovered there was some kind of a "nigger convention" going on. And how the smell made his wife sick.

Bubba's wife butted in.

"You just cain't imagine what it was like," she said.

They moved out of the hotel and Bubba said:

127

"I told the goddamn hotel manager a thing or two. He was six foot one when I started talkin' to him, but he wasn't no more than five three when I got through."

Donny Smithern laughed appreciatively, and so did the Houston wives.

With no expression, Bev said:

"I presume Blue Cross covered everything?"

The laughing stopped.

Bev then put her elbows on the table and folded her hands under her chin and said to our host, "Let me ask you a question."

She said, "If I were to bore you for, oh, half an hour about something you bitterly disagreed with, or something that irritated you, would you listen?"

Bubba put on his salesmanship smile.

"I sure would, Darlin'," he said. "But I'm not too accustomed to very many women who know that much about anything."

Donny slapped Bubba on the back. Gently.

Bev said, "I don't happen to share your feelings about the black situation."

Donny grinned.

"First of all, Beverly, it's not a situation," he said. "It's a problem. And there are a lot more niggers than there are blacks."

Bubba said, "Goddamn, you got *that* right."

One of the Houston wives said:

"I think ever-body deserves an equal chaince. But I sure don't want a bunch of niggers layin' down in the street in front of my car when I'm tryin' to go to Neiman's."

There were two very nice waiters, both black, standing behind our table, and I knew—as did Bev—that they could overhear our conversation.

I looked up at the ceiling. And I wondered, momentarily, how many "niggers" would have to lay down in the streets to keep anybody from going to a Houston Oiler game?

Bev said to Bubba not so casually:

"I don't suppose it bothers you that these waiters can hear us, does it?"

He said, "They're gonna get a hell of a tip, Darlin', so don't worry about it."

Donny said, "Niggers don't have the proper mentality. It's been proven. You never see a good nigger quarterback or distance runner. They can't think. Why do you think they're always letting somebody lead 'em into a riot?"

Bev said, "Yeah, old Martin Luther King was sure a prankster, all right."

Bubba said seriously, "Martin Luther King was responsible for *most* of the trouble this country is in *today*."

Donny said, "Damn right."

Bev said, "You're all amazing. One really shouldn't forget that there are thousands of you out there, aren't there?"

Our host said, "Just bein' honest, Darlin'. Don't I have a right to do that?"

Bev said, "Of course. But you also have an obligation to try and understand what human rights are all about."

Bubba said, "Well, let me say this about *that*. I don't

have an *obligation* to anybody but my family, my business, and my country."

Bev said, "Don't you think it's an obligation to your country, if you're interested in its future, to understand the blacks a little better. I mean, we *have* deprived them of a few things."

"Darlin', I haven't deprived 'em of a goddamn thing," he said.

"Me neither," said Donny.

"And them spooks ain't gonna deprive me of nothin'," said Bubba.

Bev said, "What in the world are you people afraid of?"

"Afraid?" Donny said. "That's crap."

Bubba sat up a little straighter and said:

"Well, Darlin', if you're gonna insist on makin' a big deal out of this, I'll tell you what I'm *concerned* about. I'm concerned that one of these days I'm gonna look around and find out that my business has been told by the Democrats that I got to hire eighty percent niggers or shut down. I'm concerned that ever high school backfield I see is gonna be darker than nighttime in Waco. And I'm concerned that ever white man's daughter is liable to wind up with V.D."

He looked around the table, immensely satisfied with himself.

Bev only smiled and said:

"That's just . . . fan . . . fucking . . . tastic."

The Houston wives fell into mild shock.

Bubba cleared his throat and said, "Now I don't know as though we need such language in here."

"Oh, okay," said Bev. "You cool it with the nigger talk and I'll cool it with the fucks. Deal?"

The Houston wives whispered something to each other.

Suddenly Beverly stood up and finished her Kahlua on the rocks. She said:

"Actually, I've got a better idea. I think I'll let you charming people have this terrific metropolis and all of its cultural splendors."

"Subversive can't take the heat, I guess," Donny said.

Bev glared at Donny.

"What'd you say, slimeball?" she said.

Donny said, "Don't call me a slimeball, you Commie."

Bev laughed.

I tried to grin. And I turned to one of the waiters and said, "Can I order a Commie well-done and hold the slime."

Bev was gone before it sank in on me that she would actually leave. I followed her out and looked all around, but a doorman finally told me he'd seen a lady get into a taxi.

"Did she have a hammer and sickle on her forehead?" I asked him.

I went back to the restaurant to tell everyone that I guessed I'd better go on back to the Executive Inn where we were staying. I was sure, I said, that Bev had gone home.

Donny said, "The damn trouble with a Liberal is, they don't want anybody else to talk."

"There's a lot of truth to that," Bubba said. "Hell, that's why I'm a Conservative. I believe in free speech

PART 2

for everybody."

Katie said, "Beverly's awfully smart. She has some good ideas about a lot of things."

Donny said to Katie, "Just mark your lip, okay?"

One of the Houston wives said:

"There's no way for anybody to total up the harm that the *media* has done to this country. It's a darn shame."

Bubba said, "Ken, I'm just sorry as I can be about this. By golly, you never know how sensitive some people are about nonsense."

His wife said, "Sweetheart, you cain't deal with her kind of attitude. She's just got a sick mind, is all she's got."

I said, well, Bev did have strong opinions about various things. I said I was sorry if this had ruined everybody's dinner.

The other wife said, "She didn't ruin mine. My rib-eye was real tender."

When I got back to the Executive Inn Beverly was in our room. She was sitting cross-legged in the middle of the bed watching television and eating a hot fudge sundae she'd ordered from room service.

I said, well, we wrapped up another joyful evening.

"What would you have liked for me to do?" she said. "Sit there and be insulted?"

I said she could have done a lot of things to make the best of it. She could have laughed a lot and put them down with glances. She could have gotten drunk. Asshole that he was, I said, Bubba was important to the tournament, and I was a golfer. She could have burned inside and taken it out on me later—as usual, I said. She

132

could have tried to change the conversation. I said she sure as hell didn't change anything those people *thought*.

She said, "Ken, do you know what a promo is?"

I said a what?

"A promo," she said. "It's a TV term."

Yeah, I said. You mean like when they tell you what's coming up tomorrow night? Like when it's third-and-goal in the Super Bowl and Captain Big Voice tells you about some silly fuckin' ice hockey game next month? I know what a promo is, I said.

"I'm going to tell you something very worldly, Ken," she said. "And I want you to remember it always."

Bev was eating a bite of her sundae when she said:

"Life . . . is a promo."

Part 3

Dump City

Five

SATURDAY AT OLD HEAVENLY PINES was certainly a unique day in the life of Kenny Lee Puckett. Only four minor things made it a different day for me than it was for two hundred million other Americans.

First, I was really getting frightened about Beverly's illness. That was the thread which kept running through everything. I mean, fuck. If a gorgeous, intelligent, thirty-one-year-old girl could come up with the Big M, then why didn't everybody else's chest hurt?

Second, I somehow jacked around and scalded that damn golf course again with a 68. And so did Donny. Same score. So there we were. Still running one-two in the National Open.

Third, because the tension and the pressure were really beginning to show on Donny and me—the publicity heat and all that—we damn near got in a fight in the locker room. Which was ridiculous. Golfers don't fist fight. They cuss a lot. But they wouldn't punch anything or anybody. They might hurt their hands and have to change their grip.

Last, Saturday was the day I found out something about Janie Ruth which would change my life again, regardless of what happened in the Open, or to Beverly, or Donny, or anybody else. I saw Janie Ruth hoist her true colors.

Donny had started making me a little hot when we had gone in the press tent again, together, Saturday afternoon. He'd pulled his phony God act for the writers.

"I believe the man upstairs will decide who's going to win this tournament," he said to the press, trying to look peaceful within himself.

He said, "All you can do is work as hard as you're physically able, prepare yourself completely, dedicate your mind and body, do the best you can, and then trust in the Lord for whatever reward will come out of it."

He said, "I'd like to win another Open, naturally. But if the grand design is for me to finish second this year, or third, or on down the line, I'll accept it graciously. And I'll be the first guy to congratulate the winner. Who I sincerely hope would be my pal, Kenny."

Somebody asked Donny if he felt that he practiced harder and longer than most everyone else on the tour in preparing for a major championship?

"I don't know of a human being who could have worked as hard for this Open as I have," he said. "Nothing else has been on my mind for the past two months. Nicklaus would probably tell you the same thing. Maybe some others. But I know what *I've* done. I know how many balls *I've* hit. I know the conversations *I've* had about it with the Lord."

I couldn't help interrupting to say, "The Lord didn't mention anything to you about what I might shoot tomorrow, did he?"

Donny refused to smile.

He gazed out at the writers and continued.

"I've got a lot to be thankful for," he said. "I've already won two major championships. That's two more than I ever thought I'd win. I've got a wonderful wife, a wonderful home. When you've been as fortunate as I've been, you can't help but know that there's something divine up there somewhere. When I recognized several years ago that God had given me the talent I have, I said to him in a prayer that it would be a crime—a dad gum *crime*—if I didn't do as much with that talent as I could. I felt that obligation then. I feel it now."

A writer asked what Donny's denomination was.

"Episcopalian," he said.

"That's a Catholic who hates calisthenics," I said.

Donny said, "That's not funny, Ken."

The writers laughed, anyhow. Most of them.

I waited until we got to the locker room before I brought up Donny's performance.

"Well, I've sure got my work cut out for me tomorrow," I said. "I got to play your low ball. You and God."

"I'll get some good print with that," Donny said.

"Doesn't it bother you at all?" I said.

"What?" Donny said.

"All that garbage down there in the tent," I said.

"Why should it bother me?" he said. "It's the truth.

139

PART 3

What do you mean *garbage?* You don't believe in God?"
I said, "Man, I'll tell you one thing. You may be the *world champion.* You wouldn't know an *Episcopalian* from an armadillo unless she flew for Delta."
"That's the church I was raised in," Donny said.
"How many times did you go?" I said.
"I don't remember," said Donny. "That doesn't have anything to do with anything. I know what I believe. I don't think it's right to talk about religion, anyhow."
"You sure as hell talked about it in the press tent," I said. "You and God are gonna win the Open. I think that's what I heard."
"I didn't say I was gonna win," Donny said.
"Who's supposed to be my partner?" I said. "Grover?"
"I didn't say I was gonna win. I said I was gonna do my best," Donny said. "I *did not* say I was gonna win. I never predict anything like that."
I said, "You left the impression—I think—that you had some kind of horse-shit *inner strength* that was going to carry you through. I been meaning to tell you this for a long time. You got any notion—at all—how funny all the guys out here think that crap is when they see it in the paper?"
Donny said, "Are you saying I'm not sincere?"
I said, "I'm saying you better make yourself some birdies tomorrow, that's all, or you're gonna belong to *me.*"
"I want to know what *you* . . . and all the other guys say about my beliefs," Donny said. "You brought it up. Let's hear it."
I said, "Oh, Lord, please let me get laid one more time this week. We thank thee, Father, for our pars on

140

the back nine. Forgive me my bogies, and those who bogey against me. Lead me not into a water hazard. For thine is the kingdom and the glory and the pussy forever. Amen."

Donny said, "You ought to have your ass whipped."

"You ought to know somebody who could do it," I said.

He took a jacket out of his locker and slammed it. He kicked a pair of shoes on the floor which belonged to somebody else.

"I'll see you on the first tee tomorrow, *friend,*" he said.

"My God," I said, feeling around on my chest and arms. "I'm healed!"

By late Saturday night at the Heavenly Marriott South I was fairly drunk when I tried to call Beverly in the hospital again. And my routine with the operator went something like this:

"Uh, Operator, this is Kenny Puckett, your National Open leader through fifty-four holes. I want to call Dallas, area code two one four. I want the Turtle Creek Medical Center where they're trying to kill Beverly Tidwell.

"What?

"Yeah, I know what time it is, Edna Merle. It's later than you know.

"How's that?

"Well, Tina Sue, then. Tina Sue. Edna Merle. Whatever you want to go by. Listen, if they give you any shit about ringing Beverly Tidwell's room at this hour, tell 'em it's an emergency.

"And, hey. Edna Tina? You need any badges tomorrow? I'd like for you and your friends to come on out to the course and watch me bring in old Donny Smithern's light-running ass.

"Old Donny Smithern's sound asleep right now, probably dreaming about winning the Open Championship of the United States. But you know what?

"I got me a one-stroke lead on that son of a bitch and he might as well be trying to catch a Roman candle.

"What'd you say, Doris?

"What'd Arnold *who* shoot?

"Arnold Palmer's not gonna win this tournament. Didn't you see his plane go over this morning? He missed the cut and went home, Thurlene. And in case you're interested, all those other gunners are too far back. Nicklaus is seven shots behind me, and Trevino and them are more than that.

"It's just down to me and Donny Smithern, is who it's down to. And we'll be paired together tomorrow.

"It's just gonna be *him* . . . *and* . . . *me*. Heads up. One on one. That's a hustler's game, Velma Liz. And I've been to *all* the big rodeos in that connection.

"Excuse me. Where's my what?

"Yeah, I've got a wife, if you want to call her that. She's in the bedroom, probably beating off with a tube of Prell, seeing as how she hasn't turned out to be worth much more than a stockroom shelf in a discount store.

"What?

"This isn't old Bev, is it? Is this Beverly? I think a man making a long-distance call at this hour of the night has a right to know whether he's talking to Dallas, Texas, or one of the twenty-five or thirty Canadian provinces. Which one of you have I got? Alaska or Portland?

"Is this Beverly Tidwell? If it is, how come you don't sound like you're dying of Big C? I thought it made some kind of noise."

By then it was Beverly, of course.

I said I was sorry it was so late, and I was also sorry I'd had a corpsman put so much Scotch down my neck. But it had been a peculiar day, I said.

Bev said she'd watched the Saturday telecast, the whole three hours and she approved of my ensemble— the white slacks and the canary shirt with the white buckled shoes.

I said, "Well, when I played good on Thursday and Friday, I was glad I saved my lead outfits for television."

Said I thought I'd go out with my red and black tomorrow. The red Sahara shirt and the black pants, with the black grained buckled shoes. Maybe a black cap.

"Leave off the cap," she said. "Caps are for all those guys who get pocket change for advertising Amana."

What if it was windy, I said? Wind was kind of a bummer for my hair.

"Let's hope it doesn't turn out to be windy," Bev said.

I said I had an idea of what Donny would wear. His basic burnt orange and light orange checkered pants, a white turtleneck, a burnt orange alpaca—even if it's as hot as it's been—and his orange-and-white snakeskin pumps.

"And I'm sure he'll have his hair rinsed and set and put on makeup," Bev said.

I said, "Hey, Bev. I want you to know something. I'm gonna play my ass off tomorrow. I'm hitting it so good I'm liable to get a ticket for speeding."

Said it was unthinkable that a man could have shot 71, 69, 68—208—on that golf course, but I'd done it. I said Nicklaus' total of 215 was probably closer to what everybody ought to be shooting.

Bev said, "I suppose it's been pretty exciting for you around there."

I said, "I've been getting a little media attention that I'm not exactly accustomed to."

Said I'd been signing autographs every time I turned around, talking into tape recorders and microphones constantly. Said *The New York Times* had swooped down on me. Said I'd found myself hanging around with the network folks. Boone Rutledge, the producer, and Bat Killian, the director, and all kinds of New York socialites.

Said the guys in the locker room had been giving me all kinds of heat as well.

"Nicklaus says my shafts are illegal," I said. "The Mex says he thinks I've broken into somebody's medicine kit and got hold of some uppers. Weiskopf says he's gonna ship me off to NASA if I don't stop driving it around the corner on No. 1."

Bev said, "And Janie Ruth has been photographed in profile, I presume? In a tank top, very low-cut, with her legs crossed, sitting on a railing of the clubhouse terrace?"

I said I'd tell her about the splendid Janie Ruth in a minute.

First, I wanted to talk about how the pressure had become mildly suffocating. You looked at your very own name up on those leaderboards out on the course, I said, and you realized this was the National Open, after all, and there were 10,000 people following you. Along with several blue coats—the USGA officials.

Now and then, I said, you would see one of those blue coats staring at you, as if he wondered what in the hell you were doing leading the tournament that Bobby Jones and Ben Hogan used to win all the time.

Said I could almost feel that the blue coats wanted to remind me that this was the oldest of America's major championships, going back to 1895, and Newport, R.I., and Horace Rawlins, and all that shit, and that it was only held every year on the toughest and best courses, like Merion and Oakland Hills and Oakmont, places where the members owned law firms and steel companies and ate boiled children for lunch, with a tossed-rulebook salad.

I said I'd discovered that if I didn't keep my poor old mind occupied on the next shot I had to hit, that I was in danger of getting a case of lockwrist. For a golfer, I said, lockwrist could be worse than Big C. If the case was severe enough, you could wind up in a cage.

I said it had really helped me on Saturday to have Grover Scomer out there in my gallery rooting for me. Grover had missed the cut, but he had stayed around to agonize with me.

I'd see him behind the ropes occasionally, I said, and he would have his fist doubled up, socking it to the air, as if to tell me to stay aggressive.

When I would pull down real good on a tee ball, and the crowd would ooo and ahhh, I could sometimes hear Grover yelling over them. He would holler:

"*Smoke*, baby!"

And when I'd be trying to cruise a shot in there with a

nine-iron or a wedge, I'd hear him again. He'd yell:
"Get tight! Get *tight!*"

I said there was a moment on the back nine when I must have looked particularly tired. I was standing on the tee, wringing wet from the humidity, opening a fresh pack of Winstons. Grover pushed through the people and got up to the ropes, right by me:

And he said in a quiet voice:

"Tempo, Kenny."

That was all he said. But it was a good reminder.

I told Bev that Grover might be more keyed up about the last round than either me or Donny.

Said he'd told me earlier Saturday night:

"Whatever happens, Kenny, do you realize that you and Donny are going to become part of the *lore* of the game tomorrow?"

"That sure helps take the pressure off," I'd said to him.

And Grover said, "Boy, I'm gonna watch every shot. I wouldn't miss tomorrow for a free roll at a nest of Swedish starlets."

I finally realized I'd been talking a hell of a long time about myself.

I said, "Hey, Bev. Considering the fix you're in, I don't think it makes much difference who wins and who loses a fuckin' golf tournament."

She said, "Of course it does, Ken. I want you to win very badly. I'm even nervous. How *about* that? But I feel a little like Grover, too. The fact that you'll be *involved* in something so special to your sport is where the real pleasure is. Do you know what I mean?"

I guess so, I said.

She said, "You'll do your best, and either you'll win or you won't. But think of tomorrow as an experience you'll have forever. So many people in the world, Ken, never come close to knowing what it's like to be near the top of their professions—even for a week or a day. Relish it, love."

I asked her if she had the same outlook on her own predicament.

She said, "You know I do, Ken. I may not win. Some people are crude enough to say that's the probability. But can I tell you something? All day and all night long I get these little jolts of excitement about the suspense. Is that crazy?"

I said, "Well, you're in the biggest ball game of all."

Then I said, "Bev, there's something to that mind-over-matter business. I've seen it in golf. I know there have been times when I wanted to make a putt, and I've practically *willed* the ball into the cup. I felt like I did, anyhow."

I said, "Of course, people say if that's true, then how come you don't make every putt?"

I explained the answer. Any putt over ten feet long, I said, was where luck took over. And sometimes even though you could stand there and feel like you knew you were going to make the shorter putt, because you'd read the break and you knew the speed, there were times when you simply didn't get a good rap on the ball.

That was technique and nerves, I said. But it all started with the mind. If the mind didn't want the ball to go into the hole to begin with, then it had no chance.

I said it was the same thing with trying to hit some

kind of a talent shot you had to invent at times. Sometimes, I said, you might find yourself under a tree, and
you need a shot that would appear halfway impossible
because it would look like you had to choke down on a
three-iron and start the ball out low, then make it come
up and get over another row of trees, and then fade or
something to reach the green.

Maybe you had never hit a shot like that before, or
quite like that, I said. So you stand there sweating over it
and you try to envision in your mind what the swing
ought to look like. You would try to "see" the shot coming off.

You couldn't just "wish" the ball would react like you
wanted it to, or "hope" it would. You had to "know" it
would.

"And if you *believe* it enough," I said, "you can make
the shot."

Bev said, "Just for the sake of conversation, Ken, what
do you do if the shot doesn't come off and you lose your
money to Spec Reynolds?"

I chuckled and said, "Aw, well, in that case, you throw
that three-iron at your electric cart, hope it breaks, and
you tell that goddamn, lousy, rotten piece of shit that it
never was worth a fuck for anything."

I sat there for a minute, listening to her laugh.

Then I said, "Aw, Bev . . . I feel so helpless. And you
sound so good to me, laughing and all. I don't know. I
feel . . . stupid, or something."

I said I wished I could figure one thing out.

"What's God so hot at you about?" I said.

She said, "Hey, Ken. Golf's not a fair game and nei-

148

ther is life. And they never were meant to be. That's in all of your philosophy books."

Nothing for a moment.

Then I went on, "Goddamn it, it's just not right. I mean, you look around you . . . and all you can see are a bunch of rich pricks running everything to their own satisfaction. None of those sons of bitches are sick that I know of."

I was beginning to get slightly overcome with a combination of cocktails and a sense of tragedy.

"All they do," I said, "is make people do things they don't want to do. Stay poor. Got to fuckin' war against somebody they don't even know."

Bev said, "They get sick, Ken. Their minds are malignant."

I said, "That's not good enough. It's not good enough for making us breathe their fuckin' air . . . for not letting us buy a drink when we want one because of what fuckin' *time* it is . . . for sending some poor son of a bitch to prison for thirty years because he smoked something that used to be legal."

Bev said, "You realize what they've done lately, don't you? You can't get a car started without fastening yourself in a harness and tearing your clothes."

"That's right," I said. "First they hid the ashtrays. Now when you put out the cigarette in the door handle and catch on fire, you have to burn to death because you can't get out of the fuckin' harness."

I said, "How come nothing ever happens to the rich pricks except they get richer and become bigger pricks and keep on fuckin' things up? Not a single one of the foul motherfuckers ever dies until he's ninety-one and *ready*—and has it all fixed up for another rich prick to take over."

She said, "That about sums it up. Wonder how we can get in on it?"

"The only two ways I know," I said, "are to be born in the East with a hyphen in your name. Or get born in the West and have some ass-hole discover oil underneath your patio in the backyard."

I said again, "Damn it, Bev, what's happening to you is so fuckin' unfair . . . It's just . . ."

I asked Bev to hold on a second, and not hang up. My throat ached.

I went into the bathroom and made myself another cocktail. Scotch and basin water in a plastic glass. I wiped the corners of my eyes and got back on the phone.

Was Bev tired of all my babble? I asked. She said she didn't have any urgent appointments, but maybe I ought to think about getting some rest.

I said if I was hungover tomorrow it would help slow down my swing, and that was good. You can't swing the club too slowly, according to all the instruction books. Fuck golf.

I had several more things to say about the captains of industry and how they were all ass-holes who were perfectly healthy and never paid any taxes. I had a word or two more about the generous deal Bev was getting from, the Old Skipper.

We finally said goodnight with unusual affection.

And it had been during the last part of our conversation that I'd gotten around to telling Bev about Janie Ruth and Donny.

After I'd left Donny and God in the locker room I went back up to the clubhouse and ran into some of the television guys. We had a cocktail and they asked me if I would like to see some taped highlights of the day's play.

We walked over into the pines to an area near the 17th green where there were three big refrigerated trucks, one of which was what the TV guys referred to as the main production "unit."

At one end of the main unit was a large panel with about ten TV screens on it, and there were chairs for people to sit in behind a control board. Somebody got on the phone, or spoke into a headset—I forget which—and asked an engineer in another part of the unit to "throw up" the golf.

I enjoyed watching myself. I thought my outfit looked merely stupendous against the backdrop of the pines. And it was fun to hear the commentators talking about how well I was swinging, considering the pressure.

When it was over the director, Bat Killian, asked me if I had time to see a twenty-minute "porno" they usually hauled around with them. Sure, I said.

The director said, "It's a little thing we got on tape by accident at Colonial this year. It's a guy you know, and a chick, out on a secluded part of the course. They're doing naughty things."

Sounded funny, I said.

The director spoke into the headset again.

"Angie," he said. "Want to throw up the Walt Disney for Kenny?"

They explained to me how they got the tape at Colonial. On Friday they had been rehearsing and while they were testing their camera positions one of the

151

cameramen covering the 15th hole was scanning around playfully trying to pick up Hold Its in the gallery so the fellows in the unit could enjoy the scenery.

They do this a lot, they told me, and they call it "hooking a barracuda," or a "honey shot," or, as a matter of fact, a "hold it."

Anyhow, it seems the cameraman suddenly zoomed in on something which struck him as a lot more interesting than a Hold It. The video tape engineer in the unit saw it on a screen and he got equally fascinated and started preserving it for history.

By now, of course, at Heavenly Pines they had done a lot of playing around with it. They had it scored with music. And they'd "rolled credits" over it. Produced by Boone Rutledge and directed by Bat Killian. That kind of thing.

They also have various voices on it, pretending to be commentators, saying, for example, "And now let's go out to the 15th and our tournament leader, Donny Smithern."

The reason they say that is because it's Donny Smithern on the tape. He's over in the woods, leaning up against one of Colonial's pecan trees, pretty much out of sight of anybody in the gallery—but not out of sight of a TV camera on a tower, obviously. And he's dead solid getting it on with a girl who's got her back turned to the camera.

Donny had completed his round for the day but there he was, back out on the course enjoying the nice weather, leaning up against the tree trunk, with the girl pressed up against him.

The tape began with Donny and the girl kissing each other vigorously, as if they were gnawing on ears of corn.

Donny had one hand on the girl's healthy tit and he had his other hand down inside the back of her tight pink shorts, which she was wearing with a halter. In a closeup of his hand inside of the tight shorts, you could see his fingers moving around to find out what mysteries might lie between the cheeks of her ass.

You couldn't really get a good look at the girl's face, even when she moved her head. So, therefore, you couldn't swear in court that you'd made a positive identification.

But if you knew her fairly well you could testify that it definitely wasn't anybody on a Saturday night primetime situation comedy.

Who it was, of course, was Janie Ruth Rimmer fuckin' Puckett.

Naturally I didn't say anything in the unit about the girl being my own wife. None of those particular TV guys knew Janie Ruth or obviously they wouldn't have been showing me the tape. They just thought it was Donny and some kind of overheated North Central Texas Hold It.

If I had said anything they would all have been embarrassed and humiliated. And anyway, I wanted to see how the damn thing came out.

As I watched it, I started thinking, well, I know Donny's pretty slick. He's been laid on a 747 with his wife only two rows in front of him. He's been laid in a courtesy car in a traffic jam in suburban Cleveland. He's been laid in a dentist's chair in the middle of a root canal while the dentist was on the phone. I wondered if he could get laid at three o'clock in the afternoon, outdoors, during a golf tournament?

It was a good thing I didn't bet any money on it.

Next thing you knew, Donny's hands finished undoing the buttons on the sides of her tight shorts, and you could see her ass wiggling, trying to help them slide down.

In a closeup, then, you could see her hands unzip Donny's faded lime slacks and remove this thing which started to rise up, and which Donny has always affectionately referred to as "the old rut iron."

Now you saw that her pink shorts had dropped to the ground, along with her panty briefs. And there she was, bare ass at three o'clock in the afternoon with the old rut iron in her hand.

The sunlight was poking through the tops of the trees, and somebody in the unit giggled and said, "Beauty shot," and everybody laughed.

I couldn't believe it was actually going to happen. I mean, they were at a *golf tournament*—and they were *standing up*.

As I had told Beverly on the phone, "I never could do it standing up, could you?"

I'd said, "You know me, Bev. If I'm not laying on my right side, I get a heart attack."

Well, it was no problem. Donny braced himself up against the tree trunk, lifted Janie Ruth up by the butt, and they dead solid went to Machine City. All through it, Donny was kissing her with his eyes open, looking around to make sure nobody might come staggering into their part of the woods looking for a beer concession.

It didn't take them very long. Looked like they went out in 31 and came back in 32—a new course record.

Now they quickly put away the old rut iron, and Janie Ruth got her togs back up where they belonged, and before you knew it, they were just a couple of folks standing there smiling and smoking a cigarette.

Donny glanced at his wristwatch and said something. They kissed. She squeezed him in the crotch, and he patted her on the ass, and they nonchalantly went off in different directions.

The music came up. Produced by Boone Rutledge. Directed by Bat Killian. And a voice said, "We'll be back with more live action from Colonial after this word about *Fun*, the feminine hygiene deodorant."

It was so late I knew Janie Ruth had gone back to the hotel in a courtesy car, leaving the Lincoln Continental for me. She was never one to wait around while I hit practice shots, or putted, or whatever. In that moment, I was thankful. As I walked through the trees toward the contestants' parking lot, all I could see was Janie Ruth's long red hair hanging down to her bare ass while she got after the old rut iron.

I don't think I ever would have hit her. I'm an inanimate object kicker, so I probably would have broken my foot on the bumper, or something. In any case, I needed the fifteen minutes it took to drive from the course to the Heavenly Marriott South.

Driving along I thought of all the days when Janie Ruth had said she wanted to go sightseeing or shopping instead of coming out to the courses where I might be playing. I wondered how many trailer camps she'd been elected queen of?

I knew of course that Janie Ruth was no angel, but I'd thought she was a few floors above all of those fly-ins I used to call Miss I. M. Port.

It didn't take long for my anger to calm itself into its usual philosophical cynicism. The healthy, non-ulcer, it-figures school of anger.

Oh, hi, there, Janie Ruth. Who'd you fuck today? The Green Bay Packers or the National Association of Warehousemen?

That kind of anger.

I found her in Carolina Cathy's buying another wagonload of bikinis.

"Where in the hell you been?" she said. "I watched the telecast in the clubhouse with Katie. Then I went in the downstairs bar and had some drinks with David and Tallie Marr. Thought you'd look in there when you left the press tent. Where you been?"

I said I'd gone down to the TV trucks. They'd rerun the show for me.

"You sure did good," she said. "I was real proud of you. I'm so excited about tomorrow."

She said, "Don't you think it's great that either you or Donny's gonna win? At least it ain't gonna be Nicklaus or Trevino again."

I suggested we go in the bar and get a drink. There was a bar just off the lobby which the hotel very wittily called The Dogleg Right.

"They showed you and Donny a lot on television," Janie Ruth said. "You sure couldn't miss old Donny in his red-on-white-on-blue."

I said old Donny was pretty hard to miss, all right.

I picked out a table for two over in a dark corner of The Dogleg Right. I wanted some privacy. And besides that, it's never wise to leave an empty chair at your table during a golf tournament.

It's awfully easy to find yourself in a conversation with one of those well-meaning bores, still wearing his clubhouse badge after sundown across town, who will join you uninvited and start asking you if you remember where the roll point was on the old Schenectady putter.

I didn't say much through the first cocktail.

She advised me that she and Katie would walk together tomorrow. They were good enough friends, she said, that the loser would be able to take it like a good sport.

I asked if she knew where Donny and Katie were having dinner?

She said that Donny's agent and business manager, Marv Doff, had flown in from New York. They were dining with Marv, she said, to chat about tax shelters and contracts.

I said it sounded to me like Donny planned on winning.

Janie Ruth said, "He's got some of the sweetest deals. Do you know that all Donny has to do is have his picture taken sitting on that power mower and they pay him $50,000 a year? He must get a ton for them cigarette ads, and he don't even smoke that brand. And there's no tellin' what he gets for that club in Arizona he represents, which he can't even pronounce."

I held up an empty glass for the waitress to see.

Janie Ruth said, "You don't seem very elated about the

Open, by the way. You ain't sick or nothin' are you?"

I said, well . . . as a matter of fact . . . it was sort of hard to be enthusiastic about anything at the moment . . . since I'd discovered that my tender companion had been practicing the ancient art of sneak-fuckin'.

She looked at me innocently and said:

"What . . . in the world . . . are you talkin' about?"

I said I was talking about my wife and one of my so-called best friends getting it on. That's all I was talking about.

"Are you jokin'?" she said. "I know you ain't drunk."

I said I was just curious. Aside from standing up, had they also done it on a horse, and in a hang glider and maybe on water skis?

"I think you've lost your mind," she said.

My fresh drink came and I motioned for a backup.

"Look," I said. "Don't gimme any bullshit. I know you and Donny have been getting it on."

"You're saying that Donny and me been goin' to bed together?" she said.

"Aw, I don't know about bed," I said. "You might have stumbled across a bed somewhere. But I can describe a pretty good scene in a grove of pecan trees."

I said all I wanted to know was how long it had been going on. How many others there'd been whose names she could remember? Or . . . if there hadn't been any others, which I seriously doubted, if she was fool enough to think Donny gave a shit about her?

"Know what I think?" I said. "I think you've been fuckin' Donny all along. Which might have made me pretty hot at one time, but which I honestly don't give a shit about. I'm just pissed off at myself, if you want to know the truth."

"You jerkoff," she said. "I don't know who's told you what, but it's a damn lie. And I don't think it speaks very highly of you to believe it."

Aw, come on, Janie Ruth, I said. Crap.

"Crap's what it is," she said. "Whatever you done heard. I've been the best wife you ever had. I don't bitch at you. I keep myself lookin' good. I put up with your moods when you play bad. You don't *deserve* me."

I laughed and said, "A good offense has always been the best defense."

She put a Winston in her teeth and picked up a book of matches off the table, and turned her head away so I couldn't light it.

"Who could have any reason to tell you that me and Donny have been slippin' around?" she asked.

I started to tell her about the tape I'd seen when this dumb son of a bitch came over to the table and shoved out his hand and said he was "Crazy Man Martin" from "Crazy Pontiac" in Raleigh.

Said we'd no doubt seen him doing his own commercials on local TV. Said there weren't many golf fans any more avid than he was. Said he was a charter member at Heavenly Pines and he'd put old Heavenly up against any course in the country. Said he wanted to buy us a drink and wish me good luck tomorrow. Said he knew most "all the boys" on the tour, and there wasn't a single one he wouldn't be proud to have for his own son.

He began to massage my shoulders, and he looked over at Janie Ruth and said:

"This is good people right here. He's gettin' kind of famous on us, but he's good people."

Then he said with a huge grin:

"But, hell, I guess we can all remember when we were just *people*."

Janie Ruth flicked some ashes off her cigarette, and she said to "Crazy Man Martin":

"My husband and I are havin' a private conversation. So why don't you jump in one of your pisshead Pontiacs and fuck off?"

"Crazy Man Martin" lost his grin. He blinked at me. I shrugged and gave him a weak smile.

He started to back away, waving timidly at us, and dissolved into the crowd at the piano bar in The Dogleg Right.

I shook my head and chuckled at Janie Ruth and said:

"You can sure make me laugh at times. It's too damn bad you're not worth trying to clean up with a washrag."

Then I asked if she remembered, by chance, where she happened to be on the afternoon of Friday, May 11, during the Colonial?

"Why?" she said.

"Just fuckin' tell me where you think you were," I said.

She thought a minute.

And she said:

"That's the day I left the course early. I never had been to the Western museum, and that's where I went."

I asked if she recalled whether she was wearing her pink shorts and a white halter that day?

"I wear that kind of thing a lot," she said. "And you like it."

So does Donny, I said.

160

"So do a lot of men, I 'magine," she said. "I never knew you wanted me to dress like a damned old nun."

I sipped my cocktail and began to describe the fine, upstanding Christian lady and tremendously talented television performer I'd seen in the tape.

I detailed several of her mannerisms, and described her outfit. I told her about the bracelet I'd noticed on her wrist, which I'd bought her. It was also possible in the tape, I said, to see the small birthmark on her left thigh.

"Stop tryin' to jack me around, Janie Ruth," I said. "I guess, by god, a man would know his own wife's hair and neck and arms and legs and clothes and jewelry. And ass and tits."

She sighed and sat there, staring at the table. Then she looked at me defiantly and said:

"And you think that girl with Donny was *ME?*"

I signed the check in The Dogleg Right and announced to Janie Ruth that I was going up to the suite and hibernate. I was headed for an hour in a tub, I said, some food, and as many Scotches as I could drink before I did a chin on the chest.

"We can discuss our futures later," I said. "But I'll guarantee you one thing. As soon as this National Open is over, your ass is no longer on scholarship."

Up in the suite Janie Ruth went into her basic pout, and tried to continue the role of the injured party. She uttered only one sentence the rest of the night. That was when they wheeled in dinner.

She said, "Shit, nobody around here could make cornbread if they had a cornbread-makin' machine."

She ate quickly and locked herself in the bedroom until morning.

Which was fine by me. For a change I had an opportunity to be alone, to relax, get pleasantly shit-faced, call Beverly later on, and mostly entertain myself with a lot of memories.

For a while I pondered the fact that I was now O-for-three on wives. O-for-three? Hell, I was O-for-life. And that was bewildering because I was one of the smarts. There wasn't anybody who could talk me out of anything on a golf course . . . who could spin me around in a card game without me knowing it . . . who could con me into an off-brand bet on a football game. I'd never bet on Baylor. So how come when you put me up against a female, you had yourself a king-sized, filter-tip sap?

It made me think of what my old pal Spec Reynolds used to say around Goat Hills. Spec always said:

"All I know is, if the smart guys are so smart, how come they're always tryin' to figure out a way to rob the dumb guys, who've already got their hands on the cheese?"

Janie Ruth's posture of innocence that night had brought to mind Joy Needham.

If Joy had ever wanted to get it on with a friend of mine, like Donny, for example, she would probably have said, "Hey, Kenny. Let's you and me and Donny and Katie smoke some dope and get some Wesson oil and have a circus maximus."

For some reason I thought of a night long ago when a group of us were sitting around Herb's Cafe drinking beer, and talking about the things we liked best in the world.

It was one of those silly conversations you lapsed into out of crushing boredom, after you had discussed all of the serious subjects. Like whether TCU's halfback with the bad knee was going to be ready in time for the Aggie game, or whether Herb really intended to go up on the price of his chicken-fried steak dinner.

Somebody said they probably would like travel better than anything, if they could figure out a way to get out of Fort Worth. Somebody else said they couldn't imagine living without Joe Garcia's Mexican food. I think I said that nothing gave me more satisfaction than hitting a golf ball.

Finally, Joy said, "I don't think anything compares with fuckin'."

Everyone sort of looked at her, and some smiled. There were maybe six of us at the table.

"Well, I'm just bein' honest," Joy said.

Waylon Needham turned to her. And he said, "Tell me this, Sis. How would you like fuckin' a nigger?"

He wasn't totally prepared for Joy's reply.

She said, "Never tried it but once."

This was news to me, too.

Joy said, "Yawl know old light-skinned Tommy Cooper? Plays drums out at the B-52 Lounge? He caught me in a weak minute not long ago. Of course, he looks almost white."

Waylon said, "Sumbitch, you better be teasin'. Because if you ain't, I know where you can find a nigger drummer tomorrow with two broken hands."

"You asked me and I told you," Joy said. "Anyhow, you've fucked worse."

Waylon's expression was what you call your sinister. He said:

"Well, I ain't my sister."

Joy said, "It wasn't Tommy's fault. I tempted him. We went out to his car during an intermission so he could smoke a marijuana cigarette and I could watch how he did it. We started playin' around, and one thing led to another."

Waylon said that instead of breaking Tommy Cooper's hands he would probably just put an ice pick in him.

I will have to take credit for saving Tommy Cooper's life. I knew him and liked him. He used to caddy some at Goat Hills.

I said, "Aw, Waylon, can't you see she's makin' sport with you? Tommy wouldn't do a thing like that. Tell him the truth, Joy."

Joy ran her hand over Waylon's crew cut and grinned and said, "I was only foolin', Big Brother. Me and Tommy never did nothin'. He's a friend, is all he is."

Waylon said, "You shouldn't jack me around like that. I could have run him through the check-out counter for no reason at all. Although I guess it don't hurt nothin' ever now and then to get rid of a nigger."

We drank our Pearl for a while, and talked about a few other stimulating things. Why the picture shows didn't change features quicker. Whether Angelo's or Sammy's had the best barbecued ribs.

"Tell you who I *did* fuck," Joy said. "I fucked Pete

Fernandez, the bartender at the Saddle Inn. And he's a
spick."

Waylon said, "You fuck him, or did he fuck you?"

She said, "Well, I thought I wanted to at first. He
looks real cool. But he ain't so gentle. So in the middle of
everthing I tried to get him to stop. But he went ahead
anyway."

Waylon drank the rest of the beer in his can of Pearl.
Then he calmly held the can up in his right hand, with
his thumb underneath and his fingers on top. He
squeezed it until it bent in half. Then he squeezed it
another way. And then a third way. And when he finished the can was about the size of a top on a jar of
peach preserves.

"That's rape," Waylon belched.

He looked around the table.

"Pete Fernandez has done raped my little sister," he
said.

Waylon glanced up at the clock on the wall of Herb's,
and he said:

"They's time for one or two more drinks at the Saddle
Inn before closin'. Think I might drop by and dust off
the furniture."

Joy said, "He carries a knife, Waylon."

And Waylon said, "He'd better."

Personally, I didn't care what Waylon might do to Pete
Fernandez. He was a small-time pimp and dance in-
structor in his off hours. Worse than that, he was sometimes a bookmaker who wouldn't always pay off. He still
owed me $100 from a Texas-Oklahoma game from two

years back. And every time I would ask him for it, he would only show me his teeth and his switchblade.

We all walked in behind Waylon and went to the bar.

Waylon said to Pete Fernandez, "How you doin' tonight, spick?"

Pete Fernandez grinned and said:

"Fine. Doin' real fine. What you dudes up to? Want a drink?"

Waylon said, "Naw, uh . . . what I come in here for, actually . . . was to see if I could find me a greasy fuckin' spick. You don't know where I could find me one of them, do you? I want to find me a greasy fuckin' spick who sleeps in the dirt, like all them other spicks. The kind that smells like the turds their whore mothers fed 'em when they was little bitty spicks. Uh, that is, when the spick whore mothers wasn't scrapin' lice off they selves."

Pete Fernandez just kept grinning.

Waylon said, "What I'm tryin' to say is, I think you're a oily motherfucker. And I want some of your spick ass. If you got any guts you'll come on outside with me . . . and bring that fuckin' old switchblade you like to hide behind."

Pete Fernandez was still grinning when he said:

"Say, Waylon. You know what? I don't hide behind that fingernail file anymore. I hide behide this, baby."

And Pete Fernandez took a .38 from under his side of the bar and shoved it right into Waylon's chest.

"You know somehin', baby?" said Pete Fernandez. "If this thing goes off, it's gonna open you up like a new supermarket. Now why don't you just back your mean ass out of here? And stay out."

DUMP CITY

I didn't think I would ever see it, but Waylon cleared his throat, took his hands off the bar, and began backing out, motioning for the rest of us to follow him.

Out on the sidewalk no one dared to say anything to Waylon. I was only hoping he wouldn't take out his frustration on me in some way. The least I figured he might do would be to wire up Pete Fernandez's car, steal it, drive it over to Fort Worth Sand & Gravel, and fill up the inside with cement.

But Waylon only stood there. And after a couple of minutes he got this look of amusement on his face, the nearest he could come to smiling.

And he said:

"You know I believe that's the first fuckin' time I ever been laughed at."

In my whole life I don't believe I ever confessed to anybody—not even Beverly later, under intense grilling—how much Joy Needham meant to me in a period of my youth back then. Certainly I never admitted it to Joy. That was about the least fashionable thing you could do.

There's something special about your first love, I think, even if it happened to be somebody like Joy, who was destined to become a whore–lady.

I haven't checked any of the modern candidates, but as far as I'm concerned, Joy Needham is the most beautiful tramp Fort Worth ever turned out.

I'm sure all of my contemporaries would agree.

She had short blond hair which she could sort of toss into place with a movement of her head. She had blue-green eyes which somehow beckoned to you. She had a

167

spectacular body which always produced the most enviable tan at Eagle Mountain Lake.

I always felt one of her great virtues was that she could get ready to go somewhere in about three minutes. Her natural beauty helped, of course. All I know is, Joy could throw on a skirt, blouse, and loafers—she never wore a brassiere or panties, naturally—shake her hair into place, hit a lick with the lip gloss, and we'd be gone.

We would be off to a movie or a bar or a party, with her looking lazily and comfortably exciting, always happy, and smelling like summer.

Joy Needham was never the kind of whore–lady who worked out of the B-52 Lounge or the Saddle Inn. The kind who wore a wig and took a man to a back booth and gave him a head job for $10 and a bottle of champagne, or took him out to the car for $25. Thirty-minute limit.

Joy was a star.

She developed a reputation as a "party girl" or a "swinger," or whatever you want to call it. She could hold her booze, she was the best dancer in town, and she had the knack for being able to play several guys at once when she hung out around some of the better joints, like the Harmony Club.

The way she worked was, she would zero in on rising young Shriners and Jaycees who would enjoy going out on the town a couple of nights a week without their wives.

She would get a fast affair going with a guy, and the first thing he knew he would be "loaning" her $100 to get the air-conditioner repaired on her Olds. Somehow, he would never get around to asking to be paid back, and Joy, of course, wouldn't volunteer it.

Next, Joy would turn up one evening very sad. She would say that her apartment had been broken into, and her stereo had been stolen, and she didn't have any insurance.

A day later the rising young Shriner or Jaycee would take Joy to lunch and "loan" her $557 to replace the stereo. Which he would also never get back.

The way she would finally—and somewhat abruptly —get rid of the guy so she could move on to another one would be very creative.

She would phone him up at the bank or roofing company or construction office where he worked, and she would say that she had to see him immediately. Could he meet her at the Harmony Club on his way to a Little League game.

And here's what she would strap on him:

She hated to face it, she would say, but the two of them had to stop seeing each other for his own "personal safety."

Then she would "confess" that she was being "kept" by a "very rich and powerful man" in Fort Worth. She would like to get out of the trap, but she was afraid of what he might do. Anyhow, all he asked was that he see her once a week, she would say. And that she didn't get "serious" with anybody.

The rich and powerful man was good to her, she would sadly admit. She couldn't complain about that. She had credit cards. He paid her rent. But he was the wildly jealous type, and she had made the stupid

mistake of mentioning the rising young Shriner or Jaycee's name to him.

And now the rich and powerful man in Fort Worth
was furious. There was no guessing what he might do,
unless they stopped seeing each other. The rich and powerful man was muttering about such things as ruining
the rising young Shriner or Jaycee's credit rating, or telling his boss that he was a known queer, or even inform-
ing his wife that he was playing around.

Well, of course, the guy would get so frightened about
his credit rating he would become permanently consti-
pated and disappear under a pile of frozen dinners.

Joy would have told him how depressed she was that it
all had to end like this because—truthfully—he had
been the first guy who ever made her come.

Eventually she romped through so many rising young
Shriners and Jaycees who knew each other that they began to compare notes. Her "gifts" suddenly tapered off.

Well, what the hell, she said. She might as well go
hard-core. The guys all still liked her because, despite
the con, she was the prettiest and dandiest piece of ass
around.

Showing a little more style, then, Joy set herself up in
a cozy, tasteful home she rented out on Byers near
Westover Hills, which is where most of the rich fuckers
in Fort Worth live. It was a small house but it had a
swimming pool, plenty of trees, and a tall fence around
everything, which made it secluded.

She once wrote me to say I would be pleased to learn
she had finally made the big time. She was getting $200
a stunt, tax free. And more than that for a "sleep over."
Said she had a bedroom that would make you want to

turn cartwheels. Every wall was a mirror, and so was the ceiling. Said she had a huge, round waterbed which was good, she said, for "quickly in the forecourt, three on two."

I called her up one time to ask why she needed money from me every so often if things were going so good?

She said it was because things seemed to always get broken at parties on football weekends, business always got bad in the summer because so many guys took their families to Colorado, and she had a very high overhead of vibrators, grass, speed, and cocaine.

"Listen," she said. "It's not cheap to keep everybody sent up—and serve those peppermint clits."

It's actually satisfying to me today to realize that, indirectly, I changed Joy's life when I gave her the money to go into the boutique. This of course was after her profits in the whore-lady business had dwindled drastically because of that trend among Fort Worth housewives toward neighborhood sport-fuckin'.

The boutique, which she and Clarice Hubbard called "Madame Curious," never really did any good because of the location. Out there on Loop 303 near Arlington. The reason, I imagined, was because they probably didn't stock enough softball uniforms and Schlitz caps.

Nevertheless, Joy was holding forth out there one day when this fellow who was just covered up with money and a good deal older than her came in, and got very much taken with her. Joe Ralph Rucker, is who it was. Joe Ralph Rucker from River Crest, Westover Hills, the Petroleum Club, Acapulco, Aspen, and Sutton Place. He went dead solid goofy over Joy Needham. He finally got him a race horse.

It was what you call your swift romance. Joe Ralph
Rucker sent his whiskey-voiced, bridge-playing wife of
twenty-two years to Dump City. He sent his kids off to
Hawaii to become rich-hippie surfing scum, he dashed
out and loaded up on leather coats, Italian loafers, and
pirate shirts. Then he hot-combed his gray hair one day,
slid a Springsteen cassette into the tape deck of his
Porshe 944 "errand car," whipped out to the boutique,
and asked Joy Needham if she would like to marry him
and become a part of Fort Worth's dynamite couple of
the year.

I was back in Fort Worth on business not long ago,
checking up on some Dairy Queens I owned a piece of,
and I went to a party one night at River Crest with some
of the "society." And I don't mind saying that it didn't
take long for me to feel like I'd been doped or something.

The women at the party were all raving about Joe
Ralph Rucker's wonderful new wife, "Joyette," and how
she had taken Fort Worth "by storm."

I heard how Mrs. Joe Ralph Rucker—the precious, entertaining, artistic Joyette—had done an incredible job
of decorating their "second home" in Acapulco, and
their "third home" in Aspen.

I heard how she had apparently been a "whiz" at the
Junior League national convention in Tarrytown, N. Y.,
recently.

Joyette, they said, had without question become the
most enthusiastic new board member of the Fort Worth
Opera Association, the Van Cliburn Competitions, and
the Jewel Charity Ball.

And nobody knew how she had found the time to do all this while she was still a volunteer guide at the museum, and seemed to go to Europe so often.

It was fortunate, I suppose, that by the time she arrived at the party, I hadn't put away so much Scotch that I would say something to blow her cover.

From the look of the blazer and the pants she wore, and all of the gold jewelry on her fingers and wrists and around her neck like dogtags, you would have guessed that she had married Bill Blass and Cartier before she got around to Joe Ralph.

Along with her slightly understated elegance, she had the coloring you don't get in a norther on the outskirts of Jacksboro. Your basic out-of-season tan, in other words. Her hair was still blond but some fag had coiffed it up for a lot of money. Her eyes sparkled. And she still had her shape. She was gorgeous.

We were introduced in a circle of people, and she hastily mentioned that we were old friends. She extended an arm which looked like it was made out of jade and emerald. I shook the hand politely, as she said:

"It's absolutely thrilling to see you, Kenneth."

Had I been drunk I might have asked her where she'd had the voice flown in from.

In the next twenty-five minutes, more or less, I found out a number of fascinating things.

I was told by Joyette that the "fun people" in Acapulco gave the most original costume parties of anybody. That the food in Brussels was every bit as exquisite as the food in Geneva, no matter what anyone might try to tell me. That I simply had to dine at The Swan in Brussels the next time I was there.

I was told that Steamboat Springs was what Aspen used to be, and that's why they were thinking of selling the chalet and building their own "domicurculums" in Steamboat. She adored her Gulfstream III, she said. She also revealed that the "animation level" of Fort Worth had risen astonishingly.

And I was told that I certainly was looking well, although a little "weightier" perhaps.

I waited patiently for a breakthrough, but it never came. And in the next twenty more minutes I found out what all had happened to her brothers, the Needhams.

If I had been pushed to bet any real money on it, I would have said that by now at least two of them were dead, one was in Huntsville or Leavenworth doing five-to-ten, one was driving a getaway car somewhere, and Waylon, probably, was still pumping gas at Texaco No. 8—and occasionally umpiring a ball game between Harder's Auction Furniture and Tiller's Electrical Supply.

Well, not quite.

Joyette filled me in on all the Needhams.

She said that J.R., who had always taken a keen interest in firearms, of course, and was rather military-minded, had become a career Air Force officer and he was presently stationed at the Pentagon.

She said Troy was a vice-president of the Republic National Bank in Dallas, lived in a lovely ranch-style house near Richardson, had three kids, and the whole family was just "cuckoo" over the Dallas Cowboys.

Buddy and James, she said, had made a fortune in the franchise business and both were "delirious" to be living in Long Beach with all their boats and motorcycles. Surely, she said, I had heard of the rage they originated—the Woogie? There must be over two hundred places now, mostly in the West, called Mex-Chink-Wop's Woogies. Which was something that looked like a chili dog but combined the flavor of a pizza, egg roll, and burrito.

And then there was Waylon. Her oldest and dearest brother, whom I most likely remembered better than the others because he was such a "rowdy" in the old days.

Well, Waylon, of course, had gone into the Fort Worth Public School System several years ago. And he had worked very hard, first at coaching, then in driver's education, and then in teaching history and study hall. And wasn't it the most happily ironic thing in the world that just recently Waylon Needham, of all people, had been appointed the new principal of Paschal High?

That's the last time I've seen or heard of Joy. Excuse me. Joyette.

One of these days I'll run into her again, I'm sure. And I hope I find her the same way. I mean it. I hope I find her still taking on Fort Worth, playing the game by Fort Worth's rules, but kicking the piss out of it.

And enjoying the greatest inside joke of us all.

Good old Fort Worth. Freight trains, used-car lots, and loan companies. Follow the river and it'll take you to a pancake house. Chug holes in the asphalt streets and mimosa trees in the St. Augustine lawns. Downtown surrounded by a ribbon of freeways. Freedom's Defenders soaring overhead and doing touch-and-gos at the air base. "Go get 'em," everybody said. "Nuke them yellow bug fuckers." The old alma mater's stadium coming up out of a horizon of live oaks and hackberries, and in purple paint on the upper deck, for all to see, a new logo: "TCU." For a time the old one had said "cTu" but I had written a letter of complaint to the *Fort Worth Light & Shopper* pointing out that you couldn't bet on the sons of bitches if they didn't know how to spell.

From the front porch of the frame house on the south side you could see the grain elevators over the tops of junkyards, tamale factories, and washeterias. And through the night you could hear the steel mill up the road dropping those big beams.

But it was good because it was all there was. Never knew anybody who didn't laugh a lot. And nobody would have swapped it for a condominium at the Blossoming Plumeria Golf, Tennis, Beach, Bath & Sauna Resort Community, Inc.

I guess the only reason you pick up a golf club at the age of nine is because you happen to find it in the garage, rusted to the color of charcoal. It gave me something to swordfight all those chickens with in the backyard when I was Errol Flynn in *The Sea Hawk*, which was Channel 11's idea of a new movie.

My dad had gone to seek his fortune in St. Louis, and my mother had gone to seek hers in Bakersfield, and that left some grandmothers, aunts, and uncles to cook the fried pies we sold to construction workers. Everybody said my daddy was a good man, he just couldn't live with my mother. They said my mother was a good woman, she just couldn't live with my dad. Nobody ever said why they couldn't live in Fort Worth. It might have

176

had something to do with their charge accounts at the department stores.

My mother wrote once to say that L.A. was better than Bakersfield because it had movie stars and better drugstores. She said I would really like Shorty, who worked at Lockheed, if I ever got a chance to meet him.

My dad wrote once to say that nobody bought much furniture in St. Louis and he was glad to see that TCU had beaten Rice. He wrote again another time to say that Detroit was not so bad, and I would probably like Irene, if I ever got a chance to meet her. She was good at rummy tile.

One day I was out in the yard hitting tin cans with the golf club and one of my uncles said I might have a natural swing. Try it this way. And here's what we call the "overlapping grip."

There's this game called golf, he said. All games are good, but golf's the one you can play your whole life.

Golf would keep you outdoors and maybe even put you next to rich folks. That was only important if something fell off of 'em you could bend over and pick up.

Everyone seemed to know a lot about sports. On Sundays when the relatives would gather at grandmother's house to eat fried chicken and drink whiskey in the kitchen, I'd hear references to Ben Hogan and Byron Nelson because they were the greatest thing to happen to Fort Worth since the good old 36th Division whipped Hitler and Mussolini and Tokyo Rose.

I'd see Hogan and Nelson on TV. They would be hitting golf balls, surrounded by people, and they wouldn't be on any kind of golf course I had ever seen in Fort Worth. The course wouldn't have small houses across the street from it, or telephone poles lining some of the fairways. And you couldn't see the summer heat coming up from it in layers, looking like amoeba.

I asked my uncle how I could get to do what Hogan and Nelson did some day? Play golf, in other words, on a course with big trees and hills and lakes—with sloping greens where the ball seemed to roll as smooth as it did on my rich aunt's carpet. My uncle said I had to practice and "want to."

There may never be a happier time in my life than the day that uncle gave me my first set of clubs—his old Tommy Armour MacGregor irons, mainly. I've had a lot of sets of woods since then but I'm using the same irons to this day. They've had every facelift there is. They've been re-ground, re-soled, thinned up, re-grooved, re-shafted, sandblasted, weighted, unweighted, lengthened, shortened, bent and caressed so many times they must feel like my poor old mind and body.

I've tried other sets, of course. But I keep going back. Like the old gal said at the high school prom at the gymnasium, "No thankee. I'm gonna dance with the one what brung me."

By the time I was fifteen years old I was going on twenty-one. I was teeing it up with the bandits like Spec and Tiny and Hope-I-Do and Willard. And a lot of others.

There was a guy at Goat Hills we called Cecil the Parachute because he lunged at the ball and he sometimes flew off the edge of elevated tees. There was Foot the Free, which was short for Big Foot the Freeloader. There was Quadruple Unreal, who seldom said anything other than, "Quadruple unreal," when anybody hit a shot. There was Moron Tom, who spoke all of his words backwards. For example, if Moron Tom said something which sounded like, "Cod-e-rac Fockledim," that was basically the pronunciation of Dr. Cary Middlecoff spelled backwards. There was Pablo the Poet, who spoke exclusively in rhymes, as in, "You're in my line, porcupine." Or, "Think I can't, Cary Grant?"

Among the other headliners were Mister Insurance, who never agreed to take a bad partner; Rain Shed, who got drowned as often as Willard Peacock; and there were Magoo, Matty, John the Band-Aid, Zorro, Jerry the Fog, Simpo, Asbestos Ernie, Pet Shop, Whip Saw, Sausage Man, Baby Slick, Spud, Hit the Silk, Diesel Oil, and Hub Caps.

There were often games with as many as twenty guys in them—three sevensomes, roughly—and everybody would be hitting at once, betting everybody else, automatic one-down presses, every combination of teams, bingle-bangle, whip-saw, do-or-don'ts, baseball, and get-evens on nine and eighteen.

It wasn't any different from most public courses. They all had their vultures, and still do.

As the weeks and months—even years—went by, the games grew crazier and more expensive. We would play from the first tee to the third green, a marathon. We'd play the course backwards. We'd play eighteen holes with only one club. We'd play out of the streets and the front yards. Tee off from the clubhouse roof. Left-handed. One-handed. Blindfolded. One-legged. We'd play in rain, snow, tornados, electrical storms—last one dead wins—or hitting all shots from moving bicycles, carts, and running.

One day a few of us made a big effort to combat the sameness of Goat Hills. We played a marathon over several city streets and through a number of neighborhoods —maybe thirty blocks in all—to the closet of my apartment and into a brown leather loafer.

I was married to Joy at the time and we had a decent enough place to live if you didn't mind some empty beer cans and articles of clothing laying around. And an ice box with a science-fiction movie going on inside of it— starring that master of suspense and chills, the Killer Bologna.

Later, when we totaled up the casualties, we found that Cecil the Parachute had been bitten by a Chow dog after he had climbed over a Cyclone fence to fetch his Spalding Dot out of somebody's fish pond. Hope-I-Do Collins had been forced to withdraw briskly into an alley and then through the back door of the Snap Brim Lounge. He had nailed a two-iron down Berry Street and broken the windshield on a yellow Plymouth. Magoo, too, had withdrawn after finding his poor old Maxfli in the mouth of an eight-year-old, from which he couldn't manage to dislodge it.

Spec and I were playing along together with the only clubs you needed for a game like this. An old blade putter for hitting off asphalt and getting good roll, and an eight-iron for trouble shots.

As it happened, we found Willard Peacock at a bus stop, thinking he knew how to beat the game.

Willard stood on a corner by the bus stop with a pitching wedge in his hand and a ball on the ground. He was facing the street, taking practice swings.

Stopping to watch Willard for a moment we found out what he was up to.

He would wait for a city bus to pull up, stop, and open the doors. Willard thought he could chip the ball inside the bus, hop in behind it, and make up a lot of distance—several blocks—in only one stroke.

His problem was that he couldn't chip good enough to get one inside the bus, especially with people always getting off.

Spec and I sat down on the grass in front of Devaney's Cleaners and watched Willard's futile efforts.

Spec finally said, "Willard, you couldn't hit the door of one of them buses if you were the driver tryin' to climb out and go home."

Willard was taking practice swings, and he said:

"If I can get one to stop long enough I can."

Spec said, "Well, I don't know nothin' about the Fort Worth Transit System, of course, but I believe I might be tempted to bet me some money on it."

Willard turned around and said, "On what?"

Spec said, "Well, let me think. What you got in your hand there? An old pitchin' wedge, ain't it?"

Willard nodded.

Spec said, "Tell you what I'm gonna do. I'm gonna give you somethin' better than Big Nigger's ribs. I'm gonna bet you that you can't even hit the *bus*. I don't care nothin' about the door."

"The bus?" Willard said. "Anybody could hit the bus."

Spec said, "I'm just gonna give you one try now. You gotta hit the next bus with that pitchin' wedge on one try."

"How much?" Willard said.

"Shit, I'll tell you what," Spec said. "I'm gonna give you $40 to $20. 'Cause I know you're gonna choke up and go sideways."

Willard squinted at Spec.

"Next bus? One try?" Willard said.

"Just hit the bus on one try with that old pitchin' wedge you're usin'," Spec said.

"You got it," Willard said, and he started taking aim with his practice swings.

Now here came the bus, groaning to a halt, only five yards from Willard. The doors, front and rear, squeaked open, as Willard waggled his club and aimed toward the middle.

Two women stepped down with armloads of groceries, then a man in a baseball uniform, then a Mexican laborer, and then an elderly lady with a package.

As the doors closed, Willard hit the shot.

A puff of dirt came up as he scooped it. But he had swung hard enough that the ball went high into the air, came down on top of the bus, bounced, and then disappeared into the street as the bus pulled away.

"That counts!" Willard shouted. "It hit the roof! Roof's part of the bus! Roof's part of the bus!"

Spec sat there on the grass in front of Davaney's Cleaners, and stuck a weed in his mouth.

"Yeah, it counts," Spec said, "if you're talkin' about hittin' the bus with a golf ball. But what I bet my money on was that you couldn't hit it with that pitchin' wedge."

Spec looked at me and said:

"I didn't see no pitchin' wedge hit no bus, did you, Kenny?"

I was compelled to agree.

Willard Peacock whimpered at first, and then he began to growl.

"Mother jeemy fuckin' cock," Willard said, becoming a light red in the face. "Prick bammer shit gobble kingy fucker turd ass bobby gump."

Willard wadded up a $20 bill and threw it on the ground.

Still blabbering, he took another golf ball out of his pocket, put it down on the ground quickly, and took a violent swing at it, knocking it over the cleaners.

"Got fuckin' ever junk spickin' fart flower bed!" Willard called after the ball.

Then he started chasing it around the corner. But suddenly he stopped. He stood there with his head drooping momentarily.

Then he took a deep breath and said to me:

"Kenny . . . Where in the hell *is* your apartment, anyhow?"

Four of us in the marathon wound up at my apartment about the same time. Spec, Big Foot, Tiny, and me. By the time all of us had managed to hit pitch shots up onto the landing of an outside staircase, and had gotten the shots to bite—and hold—on a welcome mat, and then played our way through the kitchen and into the bedroom, I think I was leading Spec by about three strokes.

"Where is it?" Spec said. "That shoe. Which way?"

Tiny said, "Can't we turn on some more lights?"

Foot said to himself, "What the shit am I doin' here? I lay 2,037."

I looked in the closet. The brown leather loafer was

just to the left of the door, laying down on its side, by a brassiere and a used Kotex.

Foot, Tiny, and I each hit bad shots that either careened off the wall in the closet and came back into the bedroom, or missed the door altogether and went under the bed.

Spec then punched a soft little chip shot which glanced off a cardboard box in the closet, hooked to the left, and went out of sight. We heard it hit the wall, and then roll. And then stop.

When we looked in the closet the ball was inside the brown leather loafer. It was probably the best golf shot I've ever seen.

"Why, lookie here," Spec said. "I done made me some kind of hole-in-one. I believe that's the luckiest thing I ever saw."

All I could think about was that Spec hadn't been around Goat Hills the day before, and the door to the apartment was never locked, and I didn't recall that my loafer had been sitting on its side, at a perfect angle for a bank shot.

I said to Spec, "I don't suppose you've ever practiced that trick before, have you?"

Spec said, "Now ain't that somethin'? Man, I guess there's no trust left anywhere in the world. How am I gonna know we're ever gonna play a silly game like this some day?"

Because he had suggested it, I remembered later.

In the early part of September one year, we were sprawled around on the porch of the Goat Hills clubhouse, watching the course turn into the color of oatmeal.

Spec was reading the *Fort Worth Light & Shopper*, and he said casually, "You know, I believe a man could make his self some money if he had his own football team."

In what way, I wondered?

Spec said, "Aw, I was just lookin' at these old scores from last night's high school games, and I don't see no score listed for the Corbett Comets."

The who, I said?

"The Corbett Comets," said Spec. "I think they got the best team in Class A. They won their first game 44-0 and they won their second game 57-0."

He looked over at me from his wicker chair on the Goat Hills porch and said, "You don't know about them twin halfbacks Corbett's got?"

I sure didn't, I said.

Spec had a sly grin. A warm grin. He was sandy-haired, sort of stoop-shouldered, and he had a round, soft, kind face. He looked harmless enough.

He grinned and said, "I'm talkin' about the Tooler twins. Ricky Ron and Dicky Don."

I said, "Spec, what the hell are you talking about?"

He said, "The team that's gonna make you and me rich."

I wanted to know where Corbett was.

Spec said, "Aw, it's wherever we want it to be. Out there in West Texas somewhere. Don't nobody around here know where all them Class A schools are except a few geology students at TCU."

We were going to invent a team, right? I said.

"Of course we'll have to let in old Jim Tom Pinch

down at the *Light & Shopper,*" Spec said. "Somebody's gonna have to see that Corbett's scores get in the paper."

Spec thought for a minute.

"Shouldn't be hard," he said. "Jim Tom appreciates a joke. Nobody reads them scores in the fine print except gamblin' degenerates."

A week later Spec came up to me at Goat Hills, giggling. He handed me the *Light & Shopper.* He pointed his finger at the list of high school football scores.

"Lookie here," he said. "Corbett 37, Consolidated Gibson 7."

A few days after that Spec showed me, with great delight, a one-paragraph story in the sports section of the paper.

The story said:

CORBETT, Tex., Sept. 28—The South Plains area is buzzing over the exploits of the Tooler twins, Dicky Don and Ricky Ron. Together they've scored 10 touchdowns in only three games and the Corbett Comets have outdistanced their opponents by 138 to 7. Corbett Coach Shug Noble says, "They not only faster'n chaparral but they real fine kids." The Toolers will test their talents this Friday night against their toughest foe thus far, the Rankin Rodents.

Spec laughed and said, "Them Toolers are gonna wear Rankin's ass out."

Which they did, of course. Something like 64-0.

I was beginning to wonder how Spec planned for us to make any money on Corbett. Nobody at Goat Hills, even Willard Peacock, was a big enough drop-case to bet on a football game where he didn't know either one of the teams.

"Parlays," Spec said. "We got to keep 'em in parlays with two legitimate winners. Them bookies ain't gonna take a bet on Corbett alone without checkin' up on 'em."

That was true. The city's best bookies were Circus Face, Little Mike, and Puny the Stroller, and none of them were retarded.

Circus Face had a huge, round face with things going on all over it. A mashed nose, crumbling teeth, part of an ear missing, and various traces of scars. But it was a happy face. He had a continual grin, and he kept the brim of his hat turned up, all around. Frequently, his hound's-tooth jackets were on fire, sizzling slowly, from his cigar ashes. Circus Coat.

He owned a tiny bar on the west side of town only so he would have a place to get phone calls. Circus Face didn't like to drink there. Too many railroad workers came in. And he didn't like the music on the jukebox.

I asked him once why he didn't change the music.

"Don't nobody complain," he said.

You would never know Circus Face was worth a lot of money, but we all knew he was. Otherwise, how could he manage to turn up at all of the big sporting events that went on? He went to the Kentucky Derby, the World Series, and the Miss America Pageant every year.

He would come back and tell us stories.

"I win the bathing suit and the congeniality," he said one day, having just returned from Atlantic City. "But I blowed the fourth, third, and second runnerups."

That was Circus Face.

Now Spec was saying that Circus Face didn't have any

respect for parlay players. That's why he'd take Corbett in a three-teamer.

"We'll put Corbett in this week with Paschal over Carter Riverside and Lubbock Tonker over Midland Vance," said Spec.

A three-team parlay paid 5-1.

We got it on with Circus Face. Paschal and Lubbock Tonker came through for us—and so did the Tooler twins.

Spec said, "You gotta love them Comets."

In another week Spec announced that we ought to consider two-team parlays. A two-team parlay only paid $2^1/2$ to 1, but we would have a bigger edge, having to select only one legitimate winner.

By now Jim Tom Pinch had become very intrigued with the Corbett Comets. He said they made his job at the *Light & Shopper* more fun. Took his mind off his salary, the typographical errors in his column, and the coal dust which poured out of the building's ventilating system and into his hair all the time.

Jim Tom began dropping in stories about the Tooler twins more regularly, and the stories got longer.

Jim Tom would call us up at Goat Hills and ask Spec or me if we would mind if he added some characters to the plot.

Spec told him, "Now don't get too fancy. We're dealin' with high finance here."

Before Corbett's "game" with Valley Reach, a story said:

CORBETT, Tex., Oct. 30—Dicky Don (Mr. Inside) Tooler and Ricky Ron (Mr. Outside) Tooler of the

Corbett Comets are side-stepping their way into the legendary annals of Texas schoolboy football. In seven games the Tooler twins have been virtually unstoppable and the fans of Scogie County are already talking about Corbett enjoying its first perfect season since the 1920's.

This Friday the Comets travel to Valley Reach for combat against the Reapers, and Corbett Principal A. J. (Hog Caller) Hughes, himself a former Corbett football hero, said he expected more than 300 fans to follow the team on its 37-mile journey.

Coach Shug Noble, who reported last week that several college recruiters were already inquiring about Dicky Don and Ricky Ron, said, "They real fine boys who keep they feet on the ground—except when they headin' for that old alumni stripe, which I like to call the goal line." Corbett is favored by 33¹/₂ over Valley Reach.

I told Spec that I thought the Tooler twins were getting a little too famous for their own good. Or ours.

He said, "Well, we'll be through with 'em after the big Thanksgiving Day game when they beat Groover."

Groover? I said, smiling.

"The Groover Gobblers," Spec said. "Them sumbitches are tough, too."

Where was Groover? I asked.

Spec said, "Aw, it's out there somewhere, pretty much of a ghost town now, since the oil play petered out in the late 1930's."

When the big game finally came around Spec and I were ahead of Circus Face by about $1,000—or $500 each. It could have been more but we'd skillfully managed to lose a couple of weeks by putting Corbett in with some dogs. Just so Circus Face wouldn't think we were total magic, and get to wondering why.

The week of the game I thought Jim Tom Pinch's fantasies got way out of hand.

On Monday a story said:

CORBETT, Tex., Nov. 24—Coach Shug Noble has pronounced his Corbett Comets as "howlin' mad" for their showdown battle with the Groover Gobblers this week, a game which will take place, ironically enough, on Turkey Day.

Coach Noble said that Dicky Don Tooler, who has gained 1,789 yards in nine games, has shaved his head for the gigantic Class A schoolboy conflict matching teams with 9–0 records.

Dicky Don, half of the blazing Tooler twins, showed up completely bald for yesterday's practice, and encouraged all of his Corbett teammates to do likewise in a massive display of dedication. Ed (Rooster) Runty, the town barber, said, "Looks like I'm faced with a sheep-shearin'."

Tuesday we had this to read:

CORBETT, Tex., Nov. 25—Ricky Ron Tooler, the other half of the Tooler twins, a famed touchdown duo on the South Plains, injured his knee yesterday as the Corbett Comets rehearsed for Thursday's chaotic melee with the Groover Gobblers.

Ricky Ron, who has gained 2,001 yards and scored 22 touchdowns in nine games this season, was taken immediately for treatment to the local clinic in Principal A. J. (Hog Caller) Hughes' G.M.C. pickup truck.

The injury was not said to be serious. However, Coach Shug Noble announced that a prayer meeting would be slated that evening on the main street of Corbett in front of Walter Virgil's Poke-E-Dot Cafe.

And then on Wednesday:

CORBETT, Tex., Nov. 26—The Corbett Comets were installed as $6^1/_2$-point favorites today over the Groover Gobblers for tomorrow's decisive game to determine the Class A schoolboy football supremacy of the South Plains.

Coach Shug Noble expressed total confidence in his Comets, largely because of the Tooler twins. Coach Noble said, "They the two finest Christian lads I've ever known and they love to hit-chee."

Coach Noble added, "Maybe I shouldn't reveal this, but Dicky Don and Ricky Ron have taken a vow. If we don't beat Groover they say they gonna saw their daddy's jeep in half."

It was learned that Groover will arrive in Corbett four hours before the kickoff on Turkey Day, and Groover's squad and fans will hold a pep rally in front of O. R. Thompson's Bean Receiving Station.

On Thursday afternoon Spec and I had our traditional Thanksgiving dinner at Herb's Cafe. Chicken-fried steak and biscuits with cream gravy—and a case of Pearl. Jim

191

Tom dropped by to discuss what we thought the score ought to be in tomorrow's *Light & Shopper*. This was the big one, after all.

"Must be halftime out there by now," Spec smiled, looking at his watch.

I said I hoped Circus Face hadn't tried to drive out there to see the game.

Spec said, "Hell, he must have $25,000 or more tied up in other things today. A&M–Texas, Tulsa–Louisville, Ole Miss–Mississippi State, Hofstra–C. W. Post . . . all of them more important conflicts. What does he care about our little old $3,000 on Corbett?"

I dropped the fork in my plate.

Three fuckin' thousand? I said.

The fork bounced—because the gravy had already started to congeal.

"Well, it's the last game," Spec said, "Circus Face took it all on Corbett. What are you worried about?"

I said, "Oh, I don't know. I guess having to *move* to Corbett if Circus Face ever finds out."

Spec said he thought the game ought to be close. Maybe 21–7 or 28–14. He also said it would really help if Jim Tom knew a way to get the score in the Dallas papers, too. Jim Tom said he could handle it.

There was nothing to do then, but relax and have a little fun talking about the scenario of the big game.

What we decided was:

Groover would jump off to a 14–0 lead because the Gobblers would secretly have Vaseline on the shoulder-pads of their jerseys, which made them difficult to tackle.

Coach Shug Noble would suffer a minor heart attack

during an emotional lecture at halftime, and have to be raced to the Corbett Clinic.

Principal A.J. (Hog Caller) Hughes would assume the coaching chores and install a whole new offense for the last two quarters. The Winged-Y, unbalanced line, center eligible.

Coach Shug Noble's wife, Ida Jo, would get on the PA system and announce that her husband was resting comfortably but that Dr. Otis (Puker) Simmons, himself a former Corbett basketball star, didn't give the old Coacher much chance to be the same again if Corbett didn't win.

The special bleachers which had been donated by O.R. Thompson's Bean Receiving Station to accommodate the Groover fans in the north end zone would collapse—injuring twenty-eight people, two dogs, and a '57 Ford two-door.

Ricky Ron and Dicky Don would finally break loose for four touchdown runs in the last three minutes, and Corbett would emerge victorious, 28–14.

On his final touchdown scamper, which would be talked about forever, Dicky Don Tooler would be so fired up and going so fast he would sprint right out of the south end of Corbett's little wooden stadium. With his head down and his legs churning, he would tear through a barbed wire fence and a field of mesquite. And still going, he would barge onto a paved section of Route 509 and collide, crazily, with a 60-mile-an-hour butane truck.

"And die as he had lived," Spec said. "Goin' for that extra yardage."

Jim Tom promised that tomorrow's "game story"

PART 3

would be considerably more authentic, with only a few
hints of fun in it.

Some fun.

I woke up to a headline in the *Light & Shopper* that
gave me a case of the dry heaves. It said:

BUBBLE BURSTS FOR CORBETT.

And then I read:

CORBETT, Tex., Nov. 28—Under dripping skies, the
sad little town of Corbett buried a legend yesterday.

The Groover Gobblers completely stifled the
famed Tooler twins, Dicky Don and Ricky Ron, and
coasted to an easy 17-3 victory over the Corbett
Comets in a battle for the Class A schoolboy football
supremacy of the South Plains.

The heavier, tougher Gobblers, aided by a sloppy
field, never allowed the touchdown twins to break
loose for one of their patented dashes. In fact, the
longest gain from scrimmage for either of the Toolers was four yards.

The Gobblers capitalized on nine Corbett
fumbles.

So frustrated was Coach Shug Noble of the Comets in the final period, he replaced the fumbling
Toolers with another set of twins, Royce and Reece
Burnham, who combined their talents to avoid a
shutout. From near midfield during a hailstorm
Royce held the ball and the one-armed Reece booted
a field goal.

Coach Noble said afterwards, in a prayer meeting
of the townspeople in the parking lot of Nolan

194

Hillard's Paint & Body Shop, "I think we can be thankful we came as far as we went."

The Tooler twins refused to see reporters.

I drove over to a drugstore to get the Dallas papers and some Rolaids. There was the score. Groover 17, Corbett 3. I called Jim Tom at the *Light & Shopper* and said what's new, *prick*?

Jim Tom swore innocence. He said he had written the "winning" story, checked it on a proof sheet, and followed it into the page form before the presses rolled. He couldn't believe anybody could have substituted stories, but of course he had gone home after the press run began. He said it was pretty funny, though, wasn't it?

I said, "Yeah, in my case, it's about a thousand funny."

I found Spec at Goat Hills.

Spec said, "Now I know it wasn't you or Jim Tom. I think Circus Face outfoxed us one way or another."

How about if Spec was in on it with Circus Face? I suggested.

"What would I do a thing like that for?" Spec said.

Aw, I said, just to have some fun and split my thousand with Circus Face when it was all over.

"There ain't no trust between people anymore," Spec said.

I said, well, all I knew was, I had to pay up. I hoped Spec did, too. We'd collected from Circus Face when we won $500 each over the last few weeks. Now we had to pay up $1,500 apiece, regardless of how it happened.

I'd bet Corbett and Corbett fuckin' well got beat. It said so in the papers.

Spec Reynolds is big rich now. A few years ago he went

195

out to Vegas and hit a bunch of licks, mostly in those poker games at The Golden Horseshoe. Then he returned to Fort Worth and opened up the best joint in the Great Southwest.

He's still there, sitting up on a hill about twenty miles outside of town. He's kind of portly now and wears a Stetson. He owns and runs a private club—Spec's—in a large, remodeled mansion with a gatehouse. Spec's got craps, blackjack, wheels, most any kind of game you want, the best steaks and ribs on the planet, a dark bar, dancing, female companionship for those customers who desire it, and the county sheriff for a good buddy.

As Spec says, "I've got ever-thing the geese want."

I was down there not so many months ago and Spec and I got to drinking and laughing about Goat Hills and all those days. I asked him again about Corbett.

I said, "Spec, you vagrant, I know one thing. One of these days I'm going to find out that you had a cousin who was a linotype operator at the *Light & Shopper* the week of the big game between Corbett and Groover."

"Aw, shit," Spec grinned. "That would have been too easy."

Was he ever going to confess, I asked, that he and Circus Face, or *somebody*, had set me up for my poor old thousand?

Spec looked at me in that sly, harmless way.

He said, "Whether I did it or not don't matter none now, does it? What's important is the thing you were privileged to learn at so tender an age."

What the hell was *that*? I said, laughing. Always take the underdog away from home with 6^1/$_2$ to 12?

And Spec said, "Lookie here, Kenny. Don't you know them Corbett Comets taught you that a man can travel far and wide—all the way to shame or glory, and back again—but he ain't never gonna find nothin' in this old world that's dead solid perfect?"

Part 4

The Big Rodeo

Six

O N SUNDAY MORNING at the Heavenly Marriott South I woke up to the romantic sound of an emery board. My head felt like a hippopotamus slept on it. My cough was right on time so I treated it with the usual Winston.

Janie Ruth was in a chair across from the couch in the living room of the suite. She was dressed. Her suitcases were in the middle of the floor.

I looked at my watch and saw that it was reasonably early. Plenty of time to recover, at least partially, and get to the course. I hadn't blown the Open on a disqualification.

"Coffee," I said hoarsely.

Janie Ruth motioned with her eyes toward a room-service tray on a table.

"Get it yourself," she said.

I made it to the table.

"Didn't they bring any cream and sugar?" I asked.

"I don't take cream and sugar," she said.

I limped to the phone and asked the lady who answered if she would like to recommend a funeral home and a minister. She said she would send up a fresh pot.

Several minutes must have passed. I smoked some more and stared at my feet. My toenails, I decided, were concealed weapons.

"Scotch sure is good," I said to myself.

Janie Ruth made a quiet noise with her throat.

"Oh, hi, there," I said, looking up. "I'm, uh . . . Norman Huddleston, a mining engineer from Santiago. You live around here?"

Not much from over that way. Your basic chilled wind from an expressionless face.

I coughed some more.

"I've got something to tell you," she said finally.

I made a time-out gesture with my hands.

"Let me guess," I said. "You cut the sleeves off my sports coats, right?"

A year before in Augusta, Georgia, during the Masters there had been this incident. Janie Ruth chose to call it an embarrassment.

We had gone to one of those parties in Augusta which are a part of the tournament week. This was a big one in an old home somebody had rented. Steaks cooking in the backyard, bars set up everywhere, maybe a hundred guests.

These parties lure all types. You'll see golfers you might recognize, and a few like me. TV celebs, sportswriting stars, assorted pro football heroes, golf equipment salesmen, corporation biggies, ad agency immortals, local nobility, a few straight-on ladies or wives—and a normal quota of hookers.

Most of the night we stayed on the edges of the party, talking to Grover Scomer, and looking at people. I had pointed out that the guys in dark blazers and plaid pants were probably from New York, the guys in white shoes and pink coats were from Florida, the guys in windbreakers were sportswriters, the guys who looked like revolutionaries were either magazine photographers or TV technicians, and the guys with long sideburns in golf shirts and double-knits were from the Charcoal-a-Go-Go Dinner Club downtown, and they brought the hookers.

Since this was Janie Ruth's first Masters party, I can't say I didn't warn her that it would mostly consist of men, and they would mostly be drunk. But she had said:

"You ain't talkin' to a schoolteacher."

The problem was that Janie Ruth, being a healthy child, looked as much like a whore–lady to a few of the guys as any of the Sandis or Mistys that the sideburns brought in to entertain some of the more affluent male guests.

The girls worked in the upstairs bedrooms, and they had been told to be sly about it. But between love affairs, like every forty-five minutes, they would be circulating, having another ginger ale, or looking for something to steal.

Janie Ruth had gotten irritated early because she

didn't get a good piece of beef in the backyard, and there wasn't any ketchup, and they also ran out of tonic.

But then a Sandi or Misty had come up to her and said:

"Honey, you workin' out of the Go-Go or the Treasure Cove?"

I remember thinking it was a combination of the Southern intellect and the tits. If you had a good body, why wouldn't you make money with it?

Janie Ruth looked at the hook and said:

"You don't have no idea how old you're gonna be in another year. I've known you all my life."

The Sandi or Misty smirked something unintelligible in her native dialect—Savannah grits—and danced away toward a group of sunburned New Yorkers who were counting their money.

It was only a moment or two later that this guy with his shirttail out swept by us and scooped up Janie Ruth by the arm. All I heard his voice say was, "Ooops, I just fell in love again." But before I realized it, he was dragging Janie Ruth up the formal staircase.

Well, I figured if there was anybody who could handle her own case it was Janie Ruth. I grinned at Grover Scomer and we went on discussing the problems of the seventy-yard bunker shot.

Janie Ruth didn't come immediately back down the stairs, however.

I guess maybe ten minutes passed. Grover and I were just getting ready to go upstairs and see what kind of an adventure she'd become a part of when here she came, down the stairs, hotter than a half-chewed jalapena.

She walked right past us in the entrance hall, straightening her dress. "Bastard," she said, and went out the front door.

A different guy had followed her down the stairs, looking mildly frantic. He came up to me and said:

"Christ, Ken, I'm sorry. He didn't know. He was just drunk."

I got the play-by-play back in our motel room. Janie Ruth said the guy with the shirttail out wheeled her into a bedroom and locked the door. Said he slapped a $100 bill on the dresser and explained that it was good luck to "upgrade" with redheads.

She said she tried to convince him she wasn't working, but he didn't believe her. Said he jumped out of his clothes and started pawing at her bosom and blabbering. Something on the order of, "Whip 'em out . . . confectionary . . . nip-o . . . sperm-o . . ."

She said he poked his joint into the rear of her dress, and started licking her on the neck. Said he wanted to know if she had any spade girl friends. And how would she like to get a little "sperm-o-rama" popped on her forehead?

Finally, she said, she got the door open and leaped into the hallway at the same time the other fellow came along. She said the naked drunk followed her into the hall with a grin on his face and his joint in his hand. And when he saw his pal he said something like:

"Suck . . . fasha gobble . . . lay a whole pile of nigger pubic . . . sperm-o-candy . . . fuckin' piss on the old navel . . . love a shit fuck tongue-o . . ."

And he fell against the wall and slid to the floor giggling.

She said the other guy stood over him and shouted:

"Holy shit! You ass-hole! This is a fuckin' golfer's wife! Holy fuckin' shit!"

Well, I said, that was all part of the Masters. I was sorry it happened, but the guy would feel worse than she did when he sobered up. And anyhow, it was humorous, I said, if you could look at it objectively.

Evidently not.

The next morning I opened my eyes in bed at the motel and found that the sleeves to one of my sport coats were slipped over my feet around my ankles. They'd been cut off at the elbow. And the sleeves to another sport coat were on my arms. As I raised up and sat there examining myself and contemplating the mind that was responsible, Janie Ruth emerged from the bathroom and said:

"You're lucky I didn't cut off somethin' else. Not that you use it so damn much anymore."

Augusta has always been kind of a shrine to me. But I guess every pro feels that way. The course is just god-awful beautiful, and it's also fair. And then there's all that Bobby Jones business. Jones built the course and started the Masters, in case you've been living in Yugoslavia for fifty years and don't know that.

It's a very exclusive tournament. There are several ways to get in it, but most of them involve winning something, so you wind up with a field that's about half the size of the other major championships. I got in the first time by winning at Pensacola. And I saw the place for the first time with Beverly.

I can remember that as we drove toward Augusta from Greensboro, where I'd played the week before, I told

Bev all about what to expect. I almost felt like I'd seen it, having heard so much about the course and the club and the atmosphere.

All of the flowers would be blossoming, I said to Bev. The azaleas, dogwood, and juniper. The wisteria vine would be climbing up the big tree right by the main section of the big white clubhouse.

From the veranda, all decorated with tables and umbrellas, I said, you can see down into the valley of the Augusta National course—dead solid emerald—winding through corridors of tall pines.

You could look out from the veranda, I said, and see the big leaderboard on the 18th fairway, and to the left, by the 10th tee, all of the cottages that were built for folks like Bobby Jones and President Eisenhower and Clifford Roberts, who'd been chairman of the tournament for over forty years.

In the clubhouse, I'd said, everyone would be talking softly. Waiters would be opening doors, and a lot of old gray-haired Masters committeemen wearing their green jackets would be telling stories about "Bob." Meaning Jones, of course.

In the Trophy Room, I said, I knew I could spend an hour just looking at Jones's old hickory-shafted clubs in a glass case on the wall. Might even sit down and have me a piece of that peach pie I'd heard about, with some Brie.

When I turned into the grounds that first time with Beverly, a real feeling of excitement came over me. There we were, driving up that long avenue of magnolias leading to the clubhouse.

I mumbled something to Bev about the fact that we'd

arrived at headquarters. Bobby Jones, I said. Walter
Hagen. Sarazen. Armour. Hogan. Nelson. Snead. Ralph
Guldahl. Craig Wood. Henry Picard. Demaret. Middle-
coff. Arnold. Jack.

Just think, I said. They've all driven up this same
road, through these same magnolias. And now us, I said.

Beverly was looking out of the window of the car, and
she said:

"Boy, the old backward, decadent South will never let
you down, will it?"

It was that same Masters where I made the mistake of
asking Bev to try and get to know some of the other
wives a little better. When we walked up to a group of
them at a table on the veranda she noticed they were all
fairly young women like herself, but they had knitting
needles and balls of yarns in their laps.

"Hi, guys," Bev said, cheerfully. "Jesus, I didn't know
the Masters was a fucking needlepoint tournament."

I left her with the wives while I went to practice, and
that evening she told me what a thrilling experience it
had been for her.

She said the major topics of conversation were diaper
rash, the differences between Holiday Inns, and how
many touring pros preferred Hydrox cookies over Oreos.

She said she'd been forced to amuse herself to keep
from dozing off. I could well imagine.

WIFE: Isn't it beautiful here?

BEV: I heard the dogwood had leukemia.

WIFE: What do you think of the tour so far, Beverly?

BEV: Oh, it's okay if you like to watch a bunch of

blond Nazis walk around in the woods with some spades carrying their shit.

WIFE: Have you gotten to know many of the players?

BEV: Are you kidding? How do you talk to an Amana hat?

WIFE: Did you enjoy Palm Springs?

BEV: It's the ding-a-ling capital of the universe. That town could bell out Helen Keller.

WIFE: Wasn't the Hawaiian Open fun?

BEV: Only if you made it to an outer island. I'd rather be the lid on a garbage can in Hanalei than the mayor of fucking Honolulu.

WIFE: Weren't those five weeks in Florida wonderful?

BEV: Take away stone crabs and what have you got besides Donald Duck and a traffic jam on Collins Avenue?

WIFE: Looking forward to New Orleans?

BEV: Yeah, I just bought a rubber suit and an oxygen mask.

WIFE: Have you met Jack and Barbara Nicklaus yet?

BEV: We're very close. They never fail to call up when we're all in Albania together.

Sometime during that week Rita Striker, one of the veranda wives, had taken me aside and in a quiet, well-meaning way had said, "Beverly's real attractive and intelligent, Kenny, but she's going to have to change her ways if she intends to have many friends out here."

I brought that up with Bev and she said:

"Rita Striker has the same hair-do she wore as a drum majorette ten years ago. And her conversation about her stupid house and kids in Orange County would put forty thousand civilians to sleep if they were running from a napalm attack."

There was one place on the tour Bev wholeheartedly enjoyed. Perversely, of course. This was La Costa, a pretty lavish spa out in southern California near the celestial retreat of La Jolla, and not far from Torrey Pines where they play the San Diego Open, which is why you stay there if you can afford it.

La Costa, which is also where they play the Tournament of Champions, is all done up in a kind of rancho-modern-Vegas-mob-chic with a fake waterfall spilling out of the parched brown hills which hide the smog San Diego claims doesn't exist.

All we ever had to do was get within sight of La Costa and Bev would start clapping her hands, thinking about all of the room fixtures, mainly the parade of sparkling shopworn divorcees in their orange bouffant wigs and their gold lamé pants and bras.

Katie Smithern said one day she didn't think any golfer's wife should ever allow her husband to go to La Costa without her. And Donny said seriously:

"It's just a resort. There's nothing to do but play golf and take a sauna."

A lot of bewitching characters come back to mind from our trips to La Costa. All of them were nicknamed by Bev, who would devote most of her time to writing things down on napkins as she people-watched.

There was "Shoulders Larue," who carried a white kitten around with her and broke the false eyelash record for the Western regionals. She confessed to Bev one afternoon that she'd had a nose job, an ankle job, her appendix scar removed, and seven husbands.

There was "April Strange," who wore a Garbo hat and carried her tennis racket with her at night, and always sat around the piano bar staring at the female vocalist and drinking a "Denver Dildo," as she called it, which was tequila, Galliano, and Fresca in a stemmed glass.

There was "Mona Motorbike," who smoked incessantly, wore a T-shirt which said "Killer Tits," dashed to the house phone every fifteen minutes, but kept winding up with the same Dodge dealer from Escondido.

There was "Sonny Stunning," a guy who had shirts unbuttoned to the waist to show off his glistening caramel chest, wore high-heeled boots, and had a face which looked like it would crack if he lowered his right eyebrow.

There were "Nonny and Moppy from Malibu." They drank champagne for breakfast. It was said that he, Moppy, had created a hit TV series about a black, robot, female white hunter. Bev decided they probably lived in a suede house and drove a gerbil-skinned Porsche.

There was "Big Alice from Little Dallas," who wore her full-length sable into the dining room at night if it got below 78 degrees outside, and who had sipped a Margarita in her day.

There was "Crash Freelance," who had a multicolored beard, wore various blends of khaki, and told Bev he was only forty pages short of completing the big novel on the textbook industry.

PART 4

There was "Aaron Mogul," a bronze, fat, bald-headed
guy who sang *My Way* frequently at his dinner table,
who bragged that he hadn't read a book since *Black
Beauty*—"So what?"—and who kept saying he had to
get back to L.A. to "straighten out this creep who thinks
he's a film maker."

There was "Dawn Somber," a willowy blond who
glided rather than walked across the floor, and who
never smiled once over a six-day period. Except when
"Aaron Mogul" handed her some money and left.

And as Beverly said one day:

"There's also Donny Smithern, you know."

The report from across the room at the Heavenly Marriott South was that my sport coats weren't worth both-
ering with, and neither was I.

What Janie Ruth had wanted to tell me Sunday morning, essentially, was that I was a sorry son of a bitch who
had neglected her and, therefore, anything she had done
with Donny Smithern was my fault as much as hers.

But now, she said, there was more to it than that.

She and Donny were in love, she said. And they were
going to be married as soon as Donny and Katie got
everything worked out with the lawyers.

It had started out as a purely sexual thing, she said,
because I drove her to it with my neglect, but they had
gradually fallen deeply and irretrievably in love.

"You may like to fuck three-woods and one-irons, but I
don't," she said.

I thanked Janie Ruth for her confession. But I said I

felt obligated to tell her as delicately as I knew how that if she thought she and Donny were ever going to be married that she was a fucking dunce.

I said, "That prick wouldn't spring for the cost of a divorce if it was a hundred percent deductible and he had a deaf-mute Raquel Welch waiting for him."

"That's all you know," she said.

I said, "Janie Ruth, I really don't care, but Donny's not about to break up his home. In planning your future, you ought to understand that. What'd he do? Give you $100 and tell you to keep dancing until the jewelry stores open in the morning?"

She said, "That home's already broke up, for your information."

Since when? I said.

"Since Katie caught us," she said.

I had to admit it. That was a stunner.

Janie Ruth explained that they had been caught at Doral. They'd sneaked off to Rita and Billy Striker's room one day while Billy and I were on the course and Rita was at the hairdresser. In their haste they'd forgotten to lock the door. Katie had come looking for Rita to ask her if she wanted to join some of the wives for a ride in the Goodyear blimp. Walked in. And there they were.

She said, "Katie took it real good. She said she knew it wasn't the first affair Donny'd ever had. She said she'd wondered about us because I talked about him so much, and I always tried to sit next to him at dinner. She wanted to know if it was serious between us? And *he* said it was."

"Naturally he said it was serious," I said. "You think he

wanted to get kicked in the ankle and have to skip Bay Hill? He could work it out with Katie later on."

Janie Ruth said, "The trouble with you is, you don't know anything about love. You don't know what it's like just to have somebody touch you and make you tingle all over."

Yeah, I do, I said. That's what happens with me and my one-iron.

Then I inquired when any of them intended to let me in on all this.

"We worried that you might already know," Janie Ruth said. "We thought maybe Katie might tell Beverly and Beverly might tell you."

That wasn't Bev's style, I said, thinking that if I ever wanted anybody to keep a secret for me I knew who to call on.

For some reason, then, I started to feel sorry for Janie Ruth. She was so dumb. And she was going to wind up the big loser.

I asked her where she was going with the bags packed.

Akron, she said, proudly. She and Donny were going to meet in Akron tomorrow and do a hideout week during the American Golf Classic at Firestone. Katie was going home.

And then what, I asked.

"He may play in the Western and then Milwaukee," she said.

I said, "Well, I'll tell you what. I'm not going to argue about money. All I want's out. You can have whatever you think's fair."

"We'll let a lawyer decide what's fair," she said.

I said fine. But if I were her I wouldn't let the lawyer

214

get too demanding or I might be tempted to show him a spicy documentary film.

"I need some travelin' money," she said.

I gave her $600 of the $700 I had in my money clip.

She revealed her travel plans. A car and driver would get her to Raleigh. She had a flight to New York, a layover, then a flight to Akron. She thought she would be in New York long enough to watch the Open telecast. In an Admiral's Club.

"And see you get your butt beat," she said.

I said, "If you want to go back to Dallas, I won't be in the apartment. I don't know exactly where I'll be. But mainly I'll be spending a lot of time at the hospital with Bev."

I told her there was plenty of money in the checking account, and of course she had a whole purse full of plastic. I said I doubted we would be seeing each other for quite a while—if ever. But I wouldn't want to think of her being stranded somewhere.

She said, "I've *been* stranded. Now I'm gettin' myself *un*stranded."

She went to the phone and asked for somebody to come get the luggage.

I said I'd better get cleaned up and wander out to the golf course. I walked to the bedroom door and stopped.

"Janie Ruth, I want to thank you, really. For doing me a favor. All I am is wiser—and still around."

And then I took one last, long, nostalgic look at those tits, and went to the shower.

At the club I sat alone for a while in a room marked "For Contestants & Press Only." Since Donny and I were

215

the last pairing of the day at 2:07 I had plenty of time to drink about eight gallons of coffee, read through the newspapers, and take three false shits.

I decided I wanted to play an old game with myself that I had always considered therapeutic. So I took out my reliable Pentel pen and wrote on the tablecloth:

KENNY PUCKETT'S LIST OF WOES,
6/21/OPEN SUNDAY.

1. The Queen of Diamonds is two up on Beverly with only three holes to play.
2. I think I'm choking on the Open lead.
3. Self-doubt sucks.
4. Donny Smithern is a wonderful human being and a great American.
5. I don't have anywhere to live.
6. Somewhere at this moment Janie Ruth has written a check for the balance of our account.
7. I'll be 35 years old in December.
8. Joy Needham is rich.
9. I have to drive to Dallas.
10. If I hit it sideways in front of 30,000 people and national television I can always stick my head in the dirt and become a radish.
11. Groover 17, Corbett 3.
12. I haven't shit in two days.
13. I'll probably play good and putt bad—or putt good and play bad.
14. Waylon Needham is a pillar of the community.
15. There's nothing I'd like to eat.
16. There's an excellent chance that nobody in the club has any fuel for my lighter.

17. The wind is going to blow my hair but Bev says I can't wear a cap.
18. "Crazy Man Martin" will want to buy me a drink if I win.
19. The pills are all gone.
20. A man who doesn't have a place to live at least ought to be allowed to shit.
21. I didn't trim the toenails.
22. MasterCard has put out a hit on me.
23. I never tried to understand Bev.
24. Here comes Grover.
25. The Skipper is laughing.

Grover put a plate of cottage cheese and fresh fruit in front of me along with a glass of iced tea. Then he tried to talk about things other than the Open Championship of the United States. A new set of irons he was trying out. What tournaments he thought he would enter the rest of the summer. How he felt like he ought to switch to a rear-shafted putter.

"You're still going to the British Open next month, aren't you?" he asked. "I may go with you. I'd sure like to see Royal St. George's. They say it's nothing but wind on all four sides."

I said it was pretty difficult for me to think beyond the next few hours. Anyhow, a lot of things depended on Beverly.

We talked a while about Janie Ruth and Donny. I showed him my list of woes.

"I can't shit," I said.

And Grover said, "That's good. That shows you're

nervous. You've got a sense of history. You're gonna become part of the lore of golf today, Son."

I said a man who can't shit tends to get testy.

Seven

ABOUT 12:45 I FIGURED it was time to don my outfit. The red shirt, the black pants, and the cleats. I got suited-up in the locker room. I took six new black gloves with me and stepped outside where my caddy, Roosevelt, was waiting with the clubs.

"Let's go put the wheels on," Roosevelt said.

I went to the practice area and hit about thirty or forty balls, taking my time. Then we walked over to the putting green. I dropped four balls on the ground and Roosevelt crouched down behind a cup about ten feet away so he could roll the balls back to me after I putted.

First, I stood there, leaning on my putter, and looked around at the scenery. I looked at the big modern club-house with hordes of people drinking on the terraces. I looked up at the American flag rippling above, and the

USGA flag flying just underneath it. I looked all across the course at the candy-striped tents and the thousands of people encircling several of the greens within my view.

I glanced over toward the 18th green at the big leaderboard which had the names of the ten low scorers through three rounds of the tournament along with their cumulative scoring totals. There was my name on top. K. Puckett. 208. Two under par.

I thought to myself, man, this is a long way from Goat Hills.

I hit a couple of putts, and then I raised up and looked back at the leaderboard. Something about it was different.

There was my name. Right. Then Donny's. D. Smithern. 209. One under. One stroke back of me. But the third name down the board was J. Nicklaus.

"*J. fuckin' Nicklaus,*" I said out loud, to nobody.

I put my hand up to shade my eyes while I squinted at the leaderboard, trying to read Nicklaus' hole-by-hole scores. His 54-hole total had been 215, seven strokes behind me, and five over par.

But now the board said he was only one over par through 61 holes. Which meant that Nicklaus, having teed off an hour earlier, had birdied four of the first seven holes on Sunday.

And he had already passed so many players so fast they must have felt like they needed to crawl under a blanket and rub their chests with Mentholatum.

While I was standing there trying to absorb the shock of Nicklaus suddenly playing himself back into the tournament there was this deafening roar from somewhere out on the course.

And I knew what had happened. J. fuckin' Nicklaus had just birdied the eighth. He was now five under on the front nine, and only two strokes back of me, and I wasn't even out there yet.

I was right. Up went the number on the big board.

"We gonna make some birdies, too," said Roosevelt.

I started hitting practice putts. And trying to convince myself that there wasn't much I could do about Nicklaus if he was going to put up some kind of a baroque goddamn number.

I couldn't play golf at all if I worried about Nicklaus. What could he shoot? A 63, maybe? No one had ever shot a lower single round in the Open.

All that was really changed was that a third party was in this thing now. It wasn't just me and Donny. And I would have to play well to beat Donny. Which was nothing new. I just had to concentrate on my own rhythm, the shots I had to hit, and trying to beat the golf course, one shot at a time.

Grover Scomer came up to me on the putting green.

"Boy," he said. "The Golden Bear's come out of hibernation."

Fuck Nicklaus, I said, stroking a putt.

Grover said, "Well, he can't keep it up. This is too tough a track."

I hit another practice putt.

"It's about 1:55, Boss," said Roosevelt.

Grover stuck out his hand.

"Fairways and greens, Son," he said.

We shook. And as we did I put my other hand up to my neck, rolled my eyes, and coughed, trying to be funny.

"Guess I'd better go try to play golf," I said.

I asked Roosevelt to stop by a concession stand and get me two packs of Winstons and a cup of something to drink—anything—just so it had ice in it.

And I immediately bumped into Katie.

"Haven't seen Donny anywhere," I said. "He didn't withdraw, did he?"

Katie said he had been on the putting green just before I was, and he had already gone over to the first tee.

I said, "Uh . . . Katie . . . listen. Janie Ruth told me what all's been going on. I just want to say I'm sorry if you've been hurt very bad. You okay?"

She said, "Oh, sure."

I couldn't resist asking her if she had bothered to mention any of these domestic thrills to Beverly.

"A long time ago, I'm afraid," she said. "Should I have told you too, Ken?"

It didn't matter, I said. What was Bev's reaction? I asked.

"She said it was what you deserved for letting the ASPCA unload a six-dollar pet on you," Katie smiled. "She said it was what *I* deserved for being a Christian."

I smiled. Then I said:

"Janie Ruth seems to believe she and Donny are going to be married. Am I losing my mind?"

Katie said, "Well, we're definitely going to separate, Ken. I've finally gotten enough sense to insist on that. But Janie Ruth's pretty far down the list."

I kept listening.

She said, "I would think that Betsy, the rich one in Tucson, is currently No. 1. And No. 2 might be Pattie, the stewardess who's based in L.A. And No. 3 is probably Linda, the hostess at the Candlelight Club in Miami Beach."

I asked Katie if Donny had any idea how familiar she was with his stable?

"Golly," she said. "I'm sure he doesn't."

Roosevelt stepped in and said, "We got to go to work, Boss."

Katie took my arm.

"Ken," she said. "Nicklaus might catch *one* of you but I don't think he can catch *both* of you."

I hugged her around the shoulders, and began pushing my way through the crowd.

When I leaned under the gallery rope and got up on the tee there was some hearty applause.

I saw Donny looking immaculate, laughing and acting "loose," in his orange on orange. He was standing there with a group of USGA officials in their blue coats, armbands, white buttoned-down shirts, red-white-and-blue striped ties, and Oxford gray slacks.

The officials all extended their hands to me. Donny and I nodded.

I put a new glove on and spit in it. Roosevelt handed me my driver and a ball.

"I'm playing Titleist 4's," Donny said.

I said I had Hogans.

We stood there and didn't say anything else for a minute.

"I think we're supposed to wish each other luck," Donny said.

"Piss on luck," I said, and walked away a few steps to look down the first fairway.

It was completely ringed with people. Way down there at a slight bend in the fairway I saw a guy in white coveralls waving a flag on a long stick. He was signaling to the officials on the tee that the group in front of us had completed the first hole, and we could tee off.

I spit in my glove again.

Now one of the USGA blue coats strolled to the middle of the tee and held up his arms, motioning politely for quiet among the fans clustered around us behind the ropes.

"Fore, please," he said firmly.

The officials stood patiently while the crowds slowly grew quiet. Now a silence fell over the tee, and it was interrupted only by the distant clinking of glasses on one of the upper terraces of the clubhouse directly behind us.

The blue coat then said:

"This is the 2:07 starting time for the fourth and final round of the 87th Open Championship of the United States Golf Association. On the tee, Donald R. Smithern . . . 72, 69, 68 . . . 209. And Kenneth L. Puckett . . . 71, 69, 68 . . . 208."

Prolonged applause.

The blue coat looked toward Donny and said, "Mr. Smithern, it's your honor, I believe."

And as the official began backing up, he said: "Gentlemen, play away."

Donny nailed his tee ball so good I would have given him a hundred dollars for it and done a right shoulder arms with the driver. He hit a low draw that stayed under the radar for about two hundred yards and then began to rise with a little tail hook which got him around the corner of the pines. Perfect spot to get home in two, which was important because the first hole at Heavenly was a par five.

He knew he'd stung it, so he could afford to swagger. As he handed the club to his caddy he grinned at some of the spectators and said:

"Didn't know if I had enough runway there for a minute, gang."

Oh, that's it, I thought to myself. Joke time. Get the folks laughing so I have to wait now until they get quiet before I can tee off.

Although everything was pretty much of a blur when I stepped up there, got set, and finally swung, I somehow hit a decent tee ball myself.

And I started walking briskly down the center of the fairway behind the flight of the ball. Roosevelt caught up with me, and I said to him:

"I don't know who's liable to win this tournament, Rose, but if my old buddy there wants to play games, I'm gonna take his young ass to Goat Hills."

Roosevelt asked me what Goat Hills was.

I told him it was a graveyard.

Donny birdied the first hole but I didn't, even though

I cold-jumped me a one-iron and put it on the green in two. The ball hit a hard spot on the front edge of the green and kicked about forty feet past the flag. There was no living way to get it down in two putts from back there.

I blew the second putt from about four feet. The ball rolled right over the hole.

Roosevelt said, "That thing didn't hit nothin' but air, Boss."

I stood there and looked up at the sky—at the Old Skipper. And under my breath I said:

"Me again, right? Man, I wish you'd come down here and play me just one fuckin' time."

The next few holes were routine pars. Donny's birdie had put him in a tie with me for the lead. At the fifth green a leaderboard told us that Nicklaus was still five under par through thirteen holes—and only two strokes back.

Donny and I hadn't exchanged a word.

On the sixth tee, however, he pulled another one of his cute stunts. Just as I came through the ball with a four-iron, at the very instant of impact, he started walking.

It's not so much that you can *see* somebody do this when you're in the middle of a swing, but you can *sense* that it's happening. And it can cause an error in your rhythm, even in that millionth of a second.

The shot turned out okay. It fluttered in there about twelve feet from the cup, in fact, but I was hot.

And as we were hiking up a slight incline toward the green, I said:

"Hey, motherfucker. I don't need any more rollout starts from you today."

Donny said, "What do you mean?"

I said, "Just move your feet when you walk between shots, that's all."

He said, "Sorry if I was too quick."

And I said, "You just start worrying about which one of your backswings I'm gonna sneeze on."

Donny putted first on the sixth green and left himself about a two-footer for a par that he couldn't take for granted. He marked his ball and I went to work on my birdie putt.

I took one glance at it and knew I probably couldn't make it. Downhill with a fuckin' righthand break.

"I can slow-play his butt, though," I whispered to Roosevelt.

I strolled all around the putt, lining it up from behind the ball and behind the cup. I did all the housecleaning I could on the line. I even pretended to flick away loose impediments that weren't there.

Roosevelt and I discussed the break and the speed at some length. I asked a photographer to move a few steps to the side. I acted like I heard an airplane overhead. In the midst of all this I noticed Donny at the edge of the green finally sitting down on his golf bag.

I backed away from the putt twice and lined it up again. And then I gave it a gentle rap.

The putt barely curled out.

I sighed and shook my head at Roosevelt. And I spent about thirty more seconds staring at the ball as it sat on the lip of the hole. I went up and raked it in for the par, and as I did I made sure I planted a shoe between the cup and the coin Donny had marked his two-footer with.

"You stepped in my line," he said, frowning.

"Aw, I'm sorry," I said. "Damn, that's gonna be on my conscience, too, if you fuck it up."

I started off the green and kept walking through an aisle of spectators toward the next tee.

When I heard the gasp of the crowd behind me I knew Donny had blown the putt.

Nothing very eventful over the next couple of holes. I got away with a bad drive on the seventh, and Donny made a good bunker shot at the eighth. I went to the ninth tee with a one-stroke lead on Donny and what I presumed to be a two-stroke lead on Nicklaus. I hadn't heard any roars from wherever Jack's gallery might be. Near the 16th, I guessed.

When I reached down to tee up my ball on No. 9 something behind me caused a distraction. It was Donny, teeing up his ball at the same time. It was my honor, of course, because he had bogied the sixth hole but he thought he'd try to put a little fast-play action on me.

I raised up and stepped over where I could look in a straight line from one tee marker across to the other. I looked at the two balls sitting on tees.

"Donny, I believe you're away," I said.

He looked at me for a second, leaning on his driver, as the fans who were up against the ropes near us giggled at the remark. Then he picked up his ball and pulled the tee out of the ground and stood aside.

The ninth is an easy driving hole. Plenty of room. The kind that makes you want to come out of your shoes at the ball. I was feeling a little cocky so as I addressed the ball I looked over at some of the people and said:

"I been hittin' shots for you people all day. I think I'll hit this one for myself."

I didn't catch it anywhere but on the screws. The ball looked like it might stay in the air long enough to send back weather reports. The crowd around the tee exploded with a cheer, and above it I heard Grover Scomer. He yelled:

"Waxahachie, Nacogdoches!"

The applause followed me all the way up the ninth fairway, even after I'd hit only a mediocre six-iron onto the green for what would be a casual four on the hole and an even par 35 going out.

Just before I arrived at the green near the clubhouse, however, my triumphant stroll was interrupted. Suddenly there was this wild bombardment of a noise, as if thousands of people at once had decided to scream. It was trailed after by an assortment of whoo-has and yeee-bo's.

Roosevelt looked at me and said:

"The Man done did somethin'."

Nicklaus, he meant.

I said, "Yeah, he's just eagled the goddamn, mother-fuckin' shit-ass 16th, I think."

Donny came up near Roosevelt and me.

"Can Jack reach 16 in two?" he said.

"Fuck, I don't know," I said. "I thought you could go to the gas chamber for playing a ball *that* hot."

Donny said, "If he made three that means he's sitting on 63 and 278. They're gonna be giving him the damn trophy when we're still out on the course."

I took a towel off Roosevelt's shoulder and wiped my face as we neared the green. And I said to Donny:

"He hasn't beaten me yet. Has he beaten you?"

We marked our shots on the green and stood there like everybody in the gallery, looking up at the leaderboard waiting for the numbers to change.

There it came. An eagle three for J. Nicklaus on the 16th.

He was seven under par for the round now, needing just two pars to finish up with a 63, a score that would tie the single-round Open record, which Johnny Miller had shot at Oakmont.

No sooner had the score for Nicklaus gone up on the board than half of our gallery went whooping off through the pines, obviously going over to watch Nicklaus.

"Run, you cunts," I said softly. "Wouldn't want any of you to miss any lore."

Donny said, "He may finish before TV even goes on the air."

"They'll have it on tape," I said. "They get a lot of interesting things on tape these days."

Donny stared at me.

Then he said:

"Kenny, we need to talk some . . . when this is over.

I'm not as heavy in all this as you think. Sure, I got it on with Janie Ruth. But I tried like hell not to . . . for a long time. I really did. If there's such a thing as self-defense in a deal like this . . ."

I said, "It doesn't matter, man."

Donny said, "I just want you to understand."

I said I understood. I had a good buddy who would fuck an alligator if it didn't have teeth. God told him to. And I'd just conveniently happened to have been married to a swamp. That was it.

He said, "I would never have done it, Kenny, if I'd thought you really loved her."

"Bat shit," I said.

"It's true," Donny said.

I said, "Hey, you know what? I can't believe I'm standing here on a golf course in the National Open talking about something like this."

He said, "She told me you two were finished. Way before I ever made a move on her. That's what she told me. I wouldn't have laid a glove on her otherwise."

I said, "Look, man, if it helps you to believe that, fine."

He said, "I'm just trying to tell you how it was."

"Swell," I said. "I appreciate it. Now you go on to Akron and fuck Janie Ruth. Right now, I'm gonna try to fuck Nicklaus."

We got away from the ninth with pars. Over the first three holes of the back side we both struggled like hell. I managed to scramble three pars out of the rough and the sand, dropping some idiot putts. But Donny bogied the

231

PART 4

10th and 11th when he sprayed two shots into bunkers so he was three strokes behind me when we got to the 13th tee. He was out of it.

The word came to us from somebody in the crowd who had a transistor. Nicklaus had *bogied* the 17th—three-putted—and parred the 18th. He finished with a 64 and a total of 279.

Now I knew what I had to do. I had a one-shot lead on the man in the clubhouse with six holes to play. I had to par them all for a 70 and a 278. I could afford one bogey and still tie. Fuck a tie. Who'd want Nicklaus in a play-off?

At the 13th tee we had to wait because someone in the group ahead of us had lost a ball. Donny and I sat beside each other on a bench inside the ropes.

We had three blue coats with us now because I was leading the tournament. And we had started collecting the writers, too. They were down the fairway on both sides, trying to be obscure in their green armbands, squatting down in groups of four, six, and eight.

It seemed silly for some reason to sit there acting like I hadn't known Donny for several years. So I said something to the grass underneath my feet.

"Katie might be a tough sell," I said. "Better phone God."

He was staring down at the ground also.

"Well," he said. "I don't know. I don't know whether I want to try to save it or not. There aren't any kids involved, fortunately. Maybe . . . I don't have any business being married. I don't suppose I'm ever gonna stop screwing around."

232

I lit a Winston off of a Winston.

"By the way," I said. "Katie knows quite a bit more than you think she does about all those shapely adorables you've got from coast to coast."

He said, "I kind of thought she might."

I said, "She's a hell of a girl, Donny."

"Yeah," he said, with a bit of a sigh. "They all are."

Over the next five holes I was in the rough twice and in the sand three times. I can't honestly remember how I gouged my way out of all that garbage. Roosevelt would hand me some kind of a club and I would take some kind of a swing and something mystical would occur.

Actually, what I was doing was stealing pars. On the 13th I hit a three-iron that was a combination half-top, half-shank, half-slice, but it wound up on the green. At the 14th my ball hit a spectator, which kept it from bouncing into a pond.

On 15 I just cold–stabbed a putt completely off-line, but it hit a cleat mark and veered into the cup. I got a free drop from an imbedded lie on the 16th, and I was in such a funk—the old "Open coma"—I damn near tried to argue the blue coat out of it.

My tee shot on the 17th hooked so deep into the trees I thought I would have to airmail my score back to North Carolina, or maybe go on a diet just to slide into the thicket to find it. But I had a clear opening to the green.

Somehow I stumbled onto the 18th tee still holding a one-stroke lead over the man in the clubhouse. And there was another fairly long wait, largely because of crowd control.

Looking down the fairway all I could see were people. And somewhere way off on the horizon, no farther away than Tibet, was the clubhouse—and the last green.

Everybody said something to me.

"You got it, Kenny," said Donny. "Just a smooth little four here. Don't get cozy. Stay aggressive."

"I got him," Roosevelt said to Donny. "I got the four for him right here. Me and my man goin' to the *house.*"

Grover had worked his way up to the ropes just behind Roosevelt.

"The dog's come and gone, Kenny," said Grover. "That dog's back there behind you somewhere."

"I got him," Roosevelt said again. "Ain't no dog in my man."

I felt like the tee ball came off the heel. But it got down there in the fairway somewhere. I remember thinking a lot of foolish things as I walked with Roosevelt toward the ball.

I thought of the old golf story about the father of the Turnesa brothers. How he had been a groundskeeper at a country club on the East Coast back in the 1920's at a time when it looked one year like his son, Joe, might win the National Open.

The old man was out on the course picking crabgrass when some members of the club rushed up to him and told him it was on the radio—Joe was winning the Open.

"Why shouldn't he?" the old man said, hardly even looking up. "All he's ever done his whole life is play golf."

That was the trouble with golf, I thought. Only a golfer could ever understand why anyone would play the stupid, fucking game.

I thought of the old story about a player named Clayton Heafner. He hated the Open, they said. Hated it because the USGA toughened up the courses so much. Made the greens slicker than the top of Sam Snead's head and narrowed the fairways so brutally you had to walk sideways down the middle of them.

All Heafner ever wanted was a one-foot putt to win the National Open so he could walk up to the ball and backhand it into the crowd. "Fuck it," he would say, and earn a lasting place in history.

I wouldn't mind having a one-foot putt to win the Open, I thought.

Roosevelt revived me. He was handing me the one-iron and saying:

"Boss, we don't need to grunt at this one. We got plenty of stick. We just need to make a good pass at it."

I didn't give myself much time to think about the shot. I just held onto the club, got comfortable, and swung as slowly as I could.

It felt good. And it looked even better.

While the ball was in flight, heading straight for the green, I slapped Roosevelt on the back, and slapped myself on the forehead.

"Goddamn, Rose," I said. "We may not even have to putt that son of a bitch."

I think that even an Egyptian mummy might have enjoyed that walk I took to the last green. I sincerely recommend the cheering for anybody's ego.

The ball was only fifteen feet from the cup. A paraplegic could have two-putted. The putt was level and almost straight. I rolled it up about six inches short of the hole, and then before it had a chance to turn into a dinosaur I calmly stepped up and rapped it in.

Almost instantly I was involved in a love tryst. First with Roosevelt, then with Donny, and then with Grover, who had scooted under the ropes and sprinted onto the green.

I didn't get a chance to throw the ball into the crowd, or make any kind of memorable gesture for television or the news photographers.

What I basically recall was Grover yelling something like, "God o'mighty, smokehouse country sausage!"

When the madness had calmed down in our little group I noticed Nicklaus standing by the scorer's tent, chatting with some USGA officials, and smiling.

We started toward each other at about the same time. And as we shook hands, I said:

"I just want to ask you one thing, Jack. What's it like to do this all the time?"

A man celebrates something stupendous in whatever way's available to him. If you're Jack Nicklaus and accustomed to such things you probably go out to an expensive restaurant with your family or a cast of business associates—or both—and you drink a few extra bottles of Chateau La-$87.50.

But if you're Kenny Lee Puckett, white man, thirty-four, you go back to your motel with Grover Scomer and

THE BIG RODEO

pour some Scotch in the trophy and get shit-faced and sing cowboy songs.

The National Open trophy is silver and it stands about two and a half feet. It has handles on it and a lid with a victory wreath on top. There's an etching on it of some ancient golfers and there are tiny engravings of all the names who have won it since 1895.

The blue coats told me the cup was actually worth about $2,500, but I don't believe it would bring that much at Winslett's Shop 'N Swap.

We sat the trophy on a table in the living room of the suite at the Heavenly Marriott South. We took off our shoes and replayed the round, and replayed the tournament, and we drank a few toasts to such people as Joe Lloyd, 1897, and Harry Vardon, 1900, and then to Bobby Jones, 1923, 1926, 1929 and 1930, and then to Ben Hogan, 1948, 1950, 1951 and 1953, and then to Jack Nicklaus, 1962, 1967, 1972, 1980.

"You know," said Grover, belching. "This isn't the original trophy. The original burned up in the fire at Tam O'Shanter in '46 when Lloyd Mangrum had it. This is a replica."

"Does it still count?" I said.

After a while we were drunk enough to think we could sing harmony. We destroyed some Jerry Jeff Walker:

It's good times when they get here
Short time til they are gone
Just pickin' and a-singin' in a family band
Travelin' and a-livin' off the land.

Then we destroyed some Billy Joe Shaver:

Like them big wheels

237

I'll be rollin'
Like them rivers
Gonna flow to sea
'Cause I'd rather
Leave here knowin'
That I'd made a fool of love
Before it made a fool of me.

When Grover had drunk and sung himself into a heap on the sofa I figured it was time to phone Beverly.

"Hi, there, broncobuster," I said. "How's life in the old bunkhouse?"

She said, "Ken, I've got to come clean. I cried. I really did. That must have been the most shattering four hours I've ever spent watching television. How in the hell can golf be so exciting?"

I said I'd hit some dumb shots. They helped along the suspense.

"It was pretty hard to see you at times," she said. "They forgot to put enough cameras in the trees."

I agreed.

She said, "Well . . . how does it *feel?*"

I said it felt fairly drunk at the moment. I said Grover was pretty funny-looking on the sofa with the National Open trophy laying on his chest.

"You don't feel immortal yet?" she said.

I said, no, I guess it took a while before a man started acting rather kingly.

She said she had some good news, too, on a minor subject.

The doctors, she said, had told her of several cases

238

where people had whipped the Big M with that linear accelerator. At least they'd licked it so far.

She said the doctors had told her about this woman in Iowa, a woman slightly older than herself who had been given only a few months. She'd had the same thing as Bev—the old grapefruit in the lung. Only worse. It had spread into both arms.

"The radiation got it," Bev said. "First, it disappeared from the arms. And then the queen of diamonds herself started to shrink. It finally went down to the size of a peanut, and they didn't even have to take it out."

That's great, I said.

She said, "They said she could live with it, and keep a close watch on it, and if it began to grow again they would take it out while it was operable. She's working now and everything. She's my idol."

"You can do the same thing," I said. "If I can win the Open just about anything is possible."

"How far are you from Dallas?" she said.

I didn't know, I said. Fifteen hundred miles. Seventeen hundred. A day and a half as the Lincoln Continental flew, I supposed. If I only stopped for a Mexican breakfast. Coffee and piss.

"How do you *look*, anyhow?" I said. "Still got the good skin?"

She said, "The only scars I have are on the inside, where they always were. My face still lights up with an alert expression when people tell me something interesting. Which is seldom. And when I was last physically active, I still had that enviable quality of being able to appear gingerly moist as opposed to sweaty and soggy."

I said I hoped she hadn't gotten skinny. She had great legs.

Bev said, "Listen, if you're thinking of coming down here and experiencing some sort of Auld Lang Syne sexual thrill, I can only submit that my body is still as sculptured and firm as it was when I won the Dallas Country Club Junior Girls' Singles. And that being stricken by senseless tragedy has only given me a strange, shadowy, erotic . . . at times mysteriously forbidden . . . and yet enticing and utterly sensuous afterglow."

Sounded fine to me, I said. Could we get the nurses to stay out of the room long enough to talk business?

"They worship me," she said. "They steal me a lot of dope. I'll just tell them to stay lost for a while, I want to get laid."

Then she said, "Hey, you know what? It would be wild. If you stop to think about it . . . with the X-ray looking down on us . . . and the crummy way a hospital smells anyway . . . and if we lifted the blinds so we could gaze out on the skyline of burgeoning Dallas . . . it would almost be like we were fucking Death."

I couldn't reply to that.

She said, "Well, Death's always fucking somebody else. I think it's time Death got fucked for a change."

I asked Bev to do me some favors. I asked her to stay funny. Stay sweet. Stay positive. I'd be there very soon to take over the chore of going out to bring her back some enchiladas.

And as we were hanging up, she said:

"Hey, old pal. Uh . . . don't have a wreck or anything.

But would you . . . like . . . you know . . . kind of hurry?"

When I was checking out of the motel early Monday morning the lobby was desolate. Emptier than a lot of hearts, as they say. The Lincoln Continental was just outside the front entrance, and a young kid in a uniform was loading my suitcases and hanger bags and golf clubs into the trunk.

The National Open trophy was sitting on the counter beside me as I signed the bill and asked the cashier to point me toward a highway in the general direction of Texas.

Grover Scomer came up. He'd thrown on some clothes and wandered down to see me off.

"Going to Akron?" I asked him.

He said yeah, he had a plane that afternoon. He said he thought he might play pretty good there. He liked the course.

I said, "Well, I'm going to Dallas. I don't know how long I'll be there."

"I guess not," Grover said.

We stood there for a moment.

I picked up the trophy and headed for the door.

"Where you gonna put it?" Grover asked.

I said, "Aw, I don't know. I probably ought to sit it up on a shelf in the Goat Hills lunchroom next to a loaf of molded bread."

Grover said, "Say, Kenny. I'll buy as many different newspapers as I can between here and Akron. I'll save 'em for you. They'd be good to look at some day."

At the door I held up the National Open trophy and admired it while Grover watched me.

"You know something, Grover?" I said. "There are a lot of people who would probably try to say that this is just about the only thing I've got in the world right now."

Grover shrugged.

I pushed open the door and looked back at him, grinning.

"That may well be true," I said. "But the damn thing's not gonna look too bad on the hood of the car, is it?"

ABOUT THE AUTHOR

*D*an Jenkins is a native of Fort Worth, Texas. For the past 23 years he has lived in Manhattan where he was a Senior Writer for *Sports Illustrated*, contributing over 500 hundred articles on the subjects of golf and football. He now writes a monthly sports column for *Playboy Magazine*, and regularly contributes articles to *Golf Digest*. His published works of fiction include *Dead Solid Perfect, Semi-Tough, Life Its Ownself, Limo* and *Baja Oklahoma*. He has also written four books of non-fiction.

Mr. Jenkins is married to the former June Burrage of Fort Worth who is the co-owner of two critically acclaimed restaurants, *Juanita's*, one located in New York City and the other in Fort Worth. Their daughter, Sally, is a sportswriter for *The Washington Post*. One son, Marty, is a TV production assistant for "Inside the PGA Tour." Their other son, Danny, is a sports and commercial photographer working with Walter Iooss Jr. in New York.